SECRETS AND MIDNIGHTS

A Deathless Love Short Story Collection

ZORA FOX

Copyright © 2026 by Zora Fox

All rights reserved.

No part of this book may be reproduced in any form or by any electronic or mechanical means, including information storage and retrieval systems, without written permission from the author, except for the use of brief quotations in a book review.

Without in any way limiting the author's [and publisher's] exclusive rights under copyright, any use of this publication to "train" generative artificial intelligence (AI) technologies to generate text is expressly prohibited.

CONTENTS

Welcome to the Eight Realms — 5
Reader Beware! — 9

1. Leaving the Party — 11
2. Obeying the Captain — 22
3. Directing the Five — 36
4. Writing the Stranger — 46
5. Luring a Sacrifice — 74
6. Predicting a Kiss — 84
7. Mounting the Siren — 98
8. Finishing the Enemy — 108
9. Craving the Enemy — 133

Thank you! — 157
Read more by Zora Fox — 159

WELCOME TO THE EIGHT REALMS

A land of gods and goddesses—a savage, beautiful collection of islands in the Corae Sea. The stories here are violent, with explicit sexual content not intended for anyone under 18. These books about deathless love feature dark, often twisted romances. Enter at your own risk.

ZENIA

Ruled by Thenios, God-King of lightning

WELCOME TO THE EIGHT REALMS

APHRISO

Ruled by Cytherea, goddess of pleasure

ERISET

Contested land, ruled by Ares and Bellona, god and goddess of war

MENOS

Ruled by Scira, goddess of wisdom

NALIA

Ruled by Basileus, god of the ocean

HYPERION

Ruled by Lox, god of the sun

KANTHAROS

Ruled by Vesta, goddess of hearth and home

FAR REALM

Ruled by Hades, god of the dead

Content warnings for these story of deathless love: listed before each story individually, but all include explicit sex (often with multiple people, monsters, or BDSM elements) and strong language

READER BEWARE!

Here's the part where I remind you that these stories are erotica. They have lots and lots of the spicy stuff we love. If you don't want to read about A) characters from the longer Deathless Love stories that might spoil the plot, or B) smut in general, turn around. This is your final warning.

In these pages, you'll encounter a variety of stories that range from the romantic to the twisted. Things these short stories have in common:

- Fantasy world—all the characters exist in the same mythology-inspired world ruled by gods and demi-gods called the deathless
- Consent, including age of consent—I'm not about non-con or truly dubious consent
- Lots of smut

That's it.
Close the door and enjoy, Foxy!

I
LEAVING THE PARTY

The human queen of Kantharos has a secret.

This original story includes explicit sex, queen and servant dynamic, quickie, and a secret relationship

Deathless hands placed the crown on my head. It was no trouble for the demi-goddess servant, since she and all the rest of the beautiful deathless were so much taller than I. It sparkled in my hair, covered in intricate nested V designs and gemstones.

In the polished bronze mirror, I saw the servant loom behind me, graceful, pale, and green eyed. Of the two of us, she looked like the queen. I had no powers. Instead, I had lines fanning from my eyes. Those facts didn't bother me unless I stood in direct comparison with any of my servants. They would outlive me. Only by their will—and particularly the goddess Vesta, may she guide and bless us with plenty—did I rule at all.

The goddess's long ago decision to appoint a human queen

in Kantharos cemented respectful treatment of all beings, whether deathless or not. I reminded myself of the privilege to serve in the capacity I did.

"Thank you," I said, picking up a cup of tea to take a sip. The hint of bitterness in the taste mirrored the bitterness that threatened at the edges of my mind. Everyone knew I held no real power. I was a role and I had play along.

Being a role and not a person for so long gnawed at my stomach some days. Today, I didn't want to be queen.

Even fetching this tea for myself earlier was a small act of rebellion. For decades, I never rebelled. My life was proper, full of bouquets and boundaries. A list of shouldn'ts. Well, I'd rebelled last week more than I ever thought I would.

I took another sip of tea.

"Will there be anything else?" asked the demi-goddess.

"No. I'll come out soon to observe the preparations for the party."

"Very good, Vesta-kori."

Her use of my queenly title was as good as my name. Until last week, I hadn't heard my true name spoken aloud in years.

She disappeared, yet another way the deathless had the power to do as they liked while I was confined by doors and walls. They usually used the doors as a matter of respect, but I didn't blame her for traveling away so quickly. This party was not only for the goddess Vesta, but also for ambassadors from beyond the Eight Realms. I had to be diplomatic. I had to be perfect.

I squinted at my reflection, new lines forming as I scrunched my nose. The goddess (may she guide and bless us with plenty) had more clout in negotiations like this, but she never participated. It was my responsibility, and the Realm would judge whether I'd done it well. The magnificent deathless weren't known for fairness.

Finishing my tea, I finally allowed my mind to wander where it truly wanted to go. Practice allowed me to continue focusing on the tasks at hand, but this week that focus had all but left me.

A glance at the door told me Ari wasn't coming. This wasn't his time to stoke the hearth—a prestigious job—or turn down my bedclothes. He'd stopped in at spare moments, but I knew not to expect him now. He was too smart for that. If he had given his distinctive, muted knock, if the door handle had turned, I wouldn't have left this room until my absence became conspicuous. We both knew it.

Drawing in a breath, I straightened my gown and exited.

The tabletop vases all had two nested V's etched into them. Good. My servants had remembered. I disliked having to remind them of anything.

Blue flowers bloomed tall in each vase, cushioned with greenery from the palace garden. They looked bright in the grand, dim hall. In less than an hour, the party would begin, the goddess Vesta herself would attend, and I would dance as carefully as possible between being queen and being human.

"Guests have begun to arrive," said a splendidly dressed decorator.

"Let me know when the ambassadors get here." There was no need to specify the same about the goddess's arrival. Everyone would know. All others would bow. I, by tradition, would stand.

"Of course, Vesta-kori."

I sent another servant to remind my twenty-year-old daughter to finish getting ready. Each small task felt as heavy as if it involved slogging through mud.

Thoughts longed to return to Ari. I still didn't see him.

I'd watched him enter my room silently for years. Of course he was handsome. They all were. His coloring was a close match for the human citizens of Kantharos: light brown. Black hair waved around his ears. His movements were precise, but with a confident carelessness that showed he'd done every task a thousand times. I liked his dimples. His skin, unlike mine, was luminous. I looked good enough for a human, but I was over forty now, an awkward age since I started to look older but still was far younger than most of the deathless. A role and not a person.

Two years ago, alone in my bedroom, loneliness had engulfed me like grief. No one knew me by my name. My coveted role left me wildly isolated. Many years ago, my daughter's father had died, but I'd never felt romantic toward him. We were cordial, not even friends. My duty to Vesta included having a daughter, so I did.

That was when I started looking forward to my small interactions with Ari. I didn't expect them to become anything more. A simple word or look was enough to bolster me for a while. But then he found more excuses to wait on me. Passing words became quick conversations. Perhaps *friend* wasn't the word, because I was queen and he was a deathless servant, but we became something similar. My stomach would surge like it used to when I was a teenager and still believed in love. The little thrill of it, waiting to hear his knock, sent me back to my room at times when I knew he was due to arrive. I started drinking tea to prevent pregnancy. It was self-indulgent to think I needed it.

Then, last week...

My mouth dried. Other places did the opposite.

I had to host this crucial party. I couldn't daydream like

this. But then I'd picture Ari's dimples, remember the way he sent pictures to my mind (his particular deathless ability) to help me sleep, recall the feel of his hands on my bare hips, and focus fell through my mind like a sieve. He made me long to be selfish. To hear him say my name.

"Helena," he moaned into my hair as he undid his trousers with one hand and cupped my lower back with the other.

Sex with my husband had never felt like this. There was none of this panting, aching need to get closer, to move together. I didn't throb for him to fill me. Now, my skin felt like it would burst with heat. That Ari wanted me like this sent me gasping. I wasn't flexible. I wasn't experienced, despite my early marriage and over forty years. Yet Ari, open mouthed, acted desperate to shove all the way inside me.

I cried out as he slid inside, too big to be comfortable. I was so tight. With small movements, he thrust in, deeper, deeper. His muscular body flexed with every motion. Dazed, I touched him. It was like a dream. My head fell back as he pressed further, letting sensation take me. I wasn't the queen —I was Helena, young and vibrant and needy.

Our first time was all heat and hands and groans. It was indecent. I hadn't realized how much I longed for indecency.

Once the barrier was breached, that we both wanted each other, the rest of the week grew even more torrid. The very memory made my heart hammer against my ribs.

I chuckled wryly. Whatever I was doing to stave off thoughts of Ari clearly wasn't working.

I checked on a few more arrangements, looking out onto the manicured garden at the guests, human and deathless. The goddess would arrive later, to be seen and lauded by all, but the ambassadors were due any minute. We had trade agreements to discuss. Northeast of Menos lay a small kingdom that boasted being the only known location for *hansou*, the soft, light fabric everyone wanted to wear in Kantharos. Without reasonable import rates, our economy would suffer. Hence, my need to negotiate with ambassadors during this party.

My mind should have been full of the important conversation ahead and of all that was at stake every time the goddess Vesta, or any other ruling deity, visited the palace.

Repeating the welcome speech to myself as I mingled among the guests, I struggled to banish the image of Ari. Maybe this was why I didn't hear about human queens acting wild like many of the deathless rulers did. It was too distracting.

A tall servant passed by with a tray of sparkling wine. Against my better judgment, I took a glass.

Vesta, may she guide and bless us with plenty, is the author of our peace here in Kantharos and for that reason and many others, we celebrate her.

My speech hit the right notes. Though the goddess rarely interacted with me personally, she had said complimentary things about my speeches in the past.

"The ambassadors are here, Vesta-kori."

The decorator had returned.

"Thank you. I'll see them now." Better to get business out of the way and move down my list of tasks. Each one completed meant one less thing to remember. One less duty separating me from another night in Ari's arms.

Many milled around the main hall now, dressed in their finest, eating and drinking. Voices grew louder as more joined the fray.

The ambassadors waited in a room adjacent to the party space. The chattering voices cut off when a servant closed the door behind us.

The male and female, both deathless as well, dipped their heads a fraction upon seeing me. Many didn't want to treat with a human queen, so their chilliness was nothing new. Pleasantries were exchanged, terms discussed.

My mind not so much wandered, but fell away from the conversation, drawn back again to the night before. Ari's mouth between my legs, his iron grip pinning my wrists to the bed, his ecstatic expression as he found release inside me... I saw it all so clearly.

My breathing shallowed as I forced my attention back to the meeting, cheeks warm.

"It's fair for both our countries, don't you think?" The man gave me a look that suggested he might have caught me daydreaming.

How mortifying.

I cleared my throat gently. "I haven't proposed higher taxes on exports from Kantharos, so I believe we still have more to discuss."

Again, I was in bed with Ari, his weight on top of me, hands over breasts, hungry kisses, his tongue in the hollow of my throat.

Clenching my teeth, I fisted my hands. Was he doing this? Sending me images?

The ambassador was still speaking, but I barely heard.

"Pardon me," I interjected as soon as he paused. "Perhaps it would be wise to bring in a third party for a fresh perspective to these issues?" Honestly, I didn't know if it would lend any clarity, but I needed to calm my mind and refocus.

I needed to find Ari. He was here, at the party somewhere.

When the ambassador looked unsure, I called over the servant at the door. "Please bring the ambassador a glass of wine. I'm afraid I must excuse myself momentarily."

Almost before I finished speaking, I was out the door. The decorated hall was hot with bodies. No sun peeked through the windows anymore. I scanned the crowd.

Ari shouldn't have sent me pictures of us together, not during this event. But my body insisted on him, despite my irritation.

There. He was already looking at me. Something told me he'd watched as I searched the room for him. With a barely there smile, he slipped through a servant's exit. As inconspicuously as I could, greeting people along the way, I followed. Checking on my servants wasn't unusual. No one would see me going into this—

Ari's hand closed around my wrist. I hadn't even shut the door. Blackness squeezed around me. Panic threatened to choke me, but Ari's grip never wavered.

With a crash, we landed in a completely different place. Brushes and fireplace tools clattered to the floor. I could barely see in this little room. We must have traveled like the deathless—disappearing in one place and arriving somewhere else. I'd never done that before.

I hadn't finished the thought before Ari was on me, pressing me back against the bank of shelves. The ache that pulsed in my dripping core spiked with urgency. "Ari!" I managed.

His fingers roughly gathered my skirt, pulling it up. "Helena."

I was feverish, finding warm ridges of flesh underneath his fine shirt.

We had minutes before people would look for me. Ari wasted no time. He held my dress in a fist, exposing me to him. As he grabbed my leg to wrap around his hip, I tugged down his pants, his ragged breath sounding loud in the dark.

This was bad, and I liked it. We worked together like a couple who had been lovers for more than a week.

A gasp forced itself out of my lungs as he entered me. Shelves pressed into my back hard enough to bruise. Tools rattled. His hot breath blew against my face. We both panted, breathless.

"Oh!" I cried, struggling to hang on to him or the shelves or anything. His fierce thrusts made me seize, almost raising me off the ground.

"Fuck, Helena," he huffed.

Heat and urgency pitched higher. He hauled my other leg up, which was more comfortable, and held my ass as he pinned me against the wall. I linked my ankles. With this improved angle, he drove in harder, deeper.

I didn't know what noises I made. Wails? I didn't sound like myself.

All I needed was more friction, more of his hard cock against my wet, aching pussy.

Shaking, I arched, involuntary. Then his hand was over my mouth as the pleasure mounted and mounted, my cries growing louder. He was hard and precise, taking control, all muscle and passion. The concentrated focus of his touch and his thrusts, burning and deep, finally built to a scream, muffled behind his hand, as I gave in completely.

He didn't take his hand away, but pushed closer, bodies together as we ground together, desperate. Finally, he let out a shuddering breath, poured hot inside me, and released my mouth. My skirt fell back into place, covering my drenched center.

He returned a moment later to kiss my lips. When my hands wandered over his sides, I found his clothes back in place too.

"Was that you?" I whispered in his ear, nipping at the earlobe. The hint of anger that remained transformed into desire. If he could have ridden me all night, I would have let him. "In the meeting room?"

He embraced me, smiling against my cheek. I felt the dimple. He was so much taller that he had to bend down to wrap his arms around me. "I couldn't resist," he said in a low voice.

"You'll have to."

We both still breathed heavily, the sound echoing in the darkness. A mess of fallen equipment lay at our feet, evidence of our desperation. I still felt it between my legs. I wanted the heat and weight of him. I wanted to be Helena.

"I'll try to wait for a better time, but I had a feeling you'd follow me," he teased, then held me tighter, lovingly. Together, we swiveled back and forth. The intimacy of it brought sharpness to my eyes.

I found his lips and lingered. By the time we broke away, we'd both caught our breath.

"Did I mess up your hair?" he murmured.

By the goddess, could he have been any sexier?

I reached up and fixed what felt like stray hairs, loose around my crowd in the mindless throb of the moment. My eyes had adjusted to see dim outlines, but no details. "You'll have to tell me."

He observed me, fixing one flyaway and tucking it around my ear.

One more time, I pulled him in by the waist, all muscle and sinew, and kissed him. "I don't want to give the speech today," I admitted. I wanted *this,* for however long it lasted.

"I know, but you give good speeches."

I laughed through my nose. "That's what they tell me."

"Just think," he said, a wicked gleam shining in his eye, "when this party is over and you've done everything you need to do, I'll be waiting to take off that dress."

I opened my mouth.

"No one will see me," he said. "I won't knock."

Fantasies engulfed me. A little breathless and very excited, I replied, "Be careful taking off the crown. I am your queen."

His answering smirk deepened that dimple. "I will use infinite care with every part of you, Helena." My name in his mouth sounded like desire incarnate.

With sigh, I held out my hand. Ari took it. In a painful blink, we were back at the accursed party.

Step by step, task by task, I'd be the queen Vesta and the rest of the Realm expected. And afterward? Afterward, I'd become Helena again as Ari, sweaty with exertion, moaned my true name into my ear.

※ 2 ※
OBEYING THE CAPTAIN

A long day of piracy calls for some controlled stress relief below deck.

Inspired by Terion and Mari's story in *Temptation and Tridents*, this story includes explicit sex, strong language, BDSM-style bondage, and the mention of violence

The *Lusca* rolled beneath us, lulling me to sleep. Through the big windows of the captain's cabin, the bright moon shone. Everything smelled like the sea and *him*.

Terion's arm slung over my waist, tucking me against his bare chest. Breathing deeply, I closed my eyes again. We had a new mission in a couple days. Getting rest was important before we made port. But with every breath, Terion's body rubbed against mine. The movements were small, but I stopped trying to ignore them. Despite being relaxing, his solid form behind me stole my thought and attention. The day had been strenuous, fixing ripped sails—Zete couldn't repair them all in the time we needed—followed by a swift meal and an unexpected merchant ship on the horizon. The captain and I determined it was headed to war-torn Eriset. The hull sported a spear design, Ares's symbol.

Was it good to antagonize the gods? Of course not. Did they need to be put in their place sometimes? Absolutely.

So we did what we did best: a violent bit of piracy. By the time we brought the loot aboard, night watches had started. Terion and I fell straight into bed.

His arm tucked around me. I curled into his body. It was comfortable.

But I always liked a challenge.

Scooting around so I lay curled to face him, I kissed his nose. Moonlight gilded his dark face, usually so gleeful and vicious. Gods, how I wanted him.

"Captain."

He blinked awake. I felt his deep breath against my belly. With a smirk, he whispered, "Nothing wrong, I hope."

I shook my head against the pillow, mussing my short hair. He fixed it, smoothing a strand back.

"I want the room."

His eyebrows shot up. "The room takes a lot of energy. Are you sure you don't want this instead?"

His hand snaked below the covers. His fingertip trailed over my side, my hip, my belly button, lower... Finally, he dipped to the spot between my legs. I squirmed against him as he teased me, rubbing with not quite enough pressure. But it was close. He'd found my neediest area right away, even through my underwear.

"This appears to suit you," he said, holding me more firmly around the back for leverage.

"No," I said, almost laughing. "Stop."

He made tighter circles with his finger.

"Constellation."

At the word, his movement halted immediately. He leaned his forehead against mine. "Do you still want the room? You know I could summon a good session if you want it." He nuzzled me, seeming thoughtful. "And I do like misbehaving around Ajax. We had a good day today."

I didn't even need to talk him into it. "Take me downstairs," I whispered. I'd seen a few instruments on the walls he hadn't used on me yet. Those would be fun. Or the reliable whips and restraints that gave me just enough discomfort to come undone when he exchanged the pain for pleasure.

He kissed my hot cheek. "You're topping from the bottom again, Terror."

"And I'll continue to do that until we begin in that room. Captain."

His answering rumble made my stomach turn liquid. "Looks like we'll have to, then." He flopped on his back before looking at the bank of windows. "Lovely night. Even if I was looking forward to uninterrupted sleep with you in my bed."

"You might have to punish me."

His crooked smile could have tamed sirens. "All right."

We heaved ourselves out of bed.

"Clothes or no clothes?" he mused.

I had on underwear, but he had nothing at all. "I doubt Ajax would appreciate us walking past him like this." Terion's first mate would be at the helm now, just outside the door. To reach the lower decks, we'd have to pass him, go across the expanse of the main deck with its towering masts, and through a door leading down.

"With bodies like ours, he would have no choice but to thank the Divine for a glimpse."

Ridiculous, but I chuckled. "Ajax has a good body too."

"Have you been looking?" He raised a brow, flashing an expression that would have looked dangerous to anyone but me. Grabbing his captain's coat and flinging it on—open, it did little to hide anything underneath—he faced me.

Before I could put on a shirt, he hooked my chin with a finger. "No one can make you scream but me." His tone was low, almost menacing, but it held promise. The patches of scales embedded in the dark skin of his cheek shimmered.

"I hope so," I replied.

He grinned wide, releasing me. His naked body visible between halves of the coat charged my pulse. He was composed of ridges as regular and dangerous as waves on the open sea. Right on his chest were more scales. He was strong everywhere. My eyes dipped to his generous cock.

After pulling on his fingerless gloves—always a feature, unless in bed or in the private room with me—he stood in the center of the room, no longer acting bleary with sleep. His face held mischief. He was thinking about what to do with me in the room.

Fuck, I loved that face.

"Ready," I proclaimed, long shirt on. I'd used this one as a dress on shore before. Tucked into pants, it completed my typical male disguise. One should always have a shirt that could blend into different personas and cultures. It had helped me more than once.

"You sound altogether too eager to lead." His smirk was teasing as he opened the door.

Ajax's broad back appeared on the deck beyond, one hand on the helm as he looked out on black ocean. He turned at the sound of the door.

If he was surprised to see the captain wearing nothing but a jacket, he didn't act like it. "Sneaking out, Captain?"

"I'm not the subtlest," he replied, spreading his arms in demonstration before wrapping one around my waist.

Ajax's lips twitched in a way that meant he was trying not to roll his eyes. "No, Captain."

Terion smiled, joy and menace. The smell and wind of the sea blew past us. The sensation of the wet, salty air always woke up his blood and mine.

We moved past Ajax. On the main deck, masts rose like towering ghosts in the light of the two lamps fore and aft.

"Friendly winds," the mate said almost begrudgingly.

"And gold on shore." Terion tossed him a wink.

We hurried to the companionway down to the lower, enclosed deck.

I used to sleep down there with the other female crew members. Memories passed by like a creature underwater. More important now was the private room.

"We should have brought a candle," I murmured as Terion opened the door, whose handle was encrusted with barnacles.

Inside, it was totally dark. We couldn't have all our fun if we couldn't see. If I'd wanted to fuck in the dark, we could have stayed in the captain's quarters.

Terion smoothed a palm down my backside. "I have plenty here, Terror."

In a matter of moments, we lit the lanterns arranged around the room. Furniture, ropes, whips, and a wall full of other instruments adorned the room. A blanket from our last encounter still lay heaped on one of the curving chairs. The air already felt warm enough to drip sweat.

Lit by appealing light from the flames, Terion faced me. "I

should be wearing more clothes," he muttered. "Make you wait."

One side of my mouth lifted. "Maybe it's good that you're naked first for once."

He lifted his chin, considering. "Word?"

"Constellation."

"Are you ready to begin?"

"Yes, Captain."

His chest rose with a slow in-taken breath, the response he always had to my submission. His lids lowered with anticipation.

"You woke me in the middle of the night," he said, voice dark as the sea.

"Yes, Captain."

"I'm nothing if not revengeful." He tilted his head. "That chair. Get on it."

"How, Captain?"

"Only answer questions." After a beat, he added, "Sit in the center, facing me." At that, he turned away, jogging his shoulders to skim off the coat. It was unfair, that back. He knew it, too.

Blood and wetness rushed between my legs. He hadn't told me to take my long shirt or underwear off, so I kept them on and did as he said. The padded chair curved, with adjustments and ties to cater to every position. I straddled the dip in the center.

"You cannot demand sessions," he said, moving forward with businesslike efficiency. If I couldn't see his throbbing hard on, I might have believed him. I bit my tongue to keep from responding.

Kneeling beside the chair, he took out loops and tightened them around my wrists. Not once did his skin make contact with mine. With each second that passed with his face close to my side and his fingers moving around mine, I yearned for that. If he moved, he could kiss my breast. He could tease the inside of my wrist with a finger not covered by his glove. Something.

Waxed leather straps closed over both wrists. When that was done, Terion hauled my arms upward, attaching them to an upper part of the chair.

"Mmm," he hummed, licking his lips. "I like you spread out for me like a meal."

I waved my knees, encouraging him to get on with it. I loved and hated these sessions. Waiting was torture—and, sometimes, so was the calculated pain he inflicted—but the release was legendary.

"No. You'll hang there. I haven't gotten my revenge yet, Terror." His dark eyes gleamed.

My breaths shortened. What did he have in mind?

He approached the wall of instruments. The trident tattoo on his forearm flashed as he took something down. It was too dim to see. His form as he returned to me was unmistakable, though. The confident swagger of someone who knew his own beauty, from his short black hair to his unbooted feet, radiated in every movement. I'd experienced that body on mine before, and I wanted it again.

I needed it again.

I swallowed back a *please*.

The objects in his hand were new. Something fuzzy and something hard, like a rock or gem. Every now and then, being teased with soft objects felt good, but Terion knew harsher methods got me off better. So what was he doing?

Instead of explaining, he set the items to the side and

raised my shirt to expose my breasts. They ended in stiff points. He gave the barest smile at the sight of them.

"Comfortable?" he asked carelessly, straightening.

I considered my answer. "No, Captain."

His brows lowered, eyes darting to the restraints keeping my arms above my head. "You have bruises. From today?"

"Yes, Captain."

"From whom?"

"One of Ares's, Captain. He's dead now."

"Good." His hand lifted to the place where he sometimes still wore the severed finger of my ex. "Why are you not comfortable?"

"Because I want to know what that does, Captain. And I want you to fuck me."

"Needy." His eyes twinkled. Reaching again for the two objects, he rubbed them together. "This is an experiment, and I prefer to experiment on you."

His arms flexed with the rubbing motion. He should have been rubbing something else...

Zap!

Terion reached for my nipple and a current shocked through my body at the contact. It wasn't only that Terion had touched me. An actual spark had zinged my skin.

He did it again on the other side. It left me breathless and braced.

"Wool," he finally said. That didn't explain much to me. "Should I shock you somewhere else?"

I was already so wet that any stimulation sounded necessary. "Yes, Captain."

"Where?"

"You know where."

He shocked my nipple again.

"Captain," I amended. "My clit, Captain."

"I wonder..." He examined my body. He'd explored every particle of it, wrapping himself in and around me, pushing my boundaries to the brink.

He rubbed the wool against the stone again and touched the cloth of my underwear. The result was surprising, but not stimulating.

"No," he said, putting it away again and taking down something else. I recognized that chain. It was one of my favorite devices. Next to it was the new toy we'd never used: a strappy, phallic thing. I'd find a way to ask about it.

Without removing his gloves, he pulled my underwear down far enough to root around and find my swollen clit. On went the metal clip attached to the chain.

I gasped and arched. No relief was possible.

Stepping away, holding the end of the chain, he tugged.

I squawked.

His face, when I could focus again, was wicked. "I told you I'd get my revenge, Mari." He pulled again.

My vision went white. I squirmed, dripping, against the seat.

"Please!" burst from my lips before I could stop it.

He teased the chain in a rhythm that left me trembling and sweating. "You will refer to me as Captain," he said smoothly.

"Achhhh! Captain!"

Clips tightened around my hard nipples.

I screamed, air coming in sobs.

"To the edge." He patted my hip.

I moved jerkily to scoot myself forward. Since I sat in the divot, I had to angle uphill, something that felt nearly impossible with a clamp on my clit and two on my nipples. I forced my way forward, refusing to lose a challenge. The tension on my wrists grew as I pulled forward.

Catching my breath, I peeled open my eyes. Terion stared at me with open lust. He was magnificent. Shit. My desire crested.

His gloves came off. "That's barely enough punishment for you," he said in a low voice. "Do you think it's enough?"

"Yes, Captain!"

"Do you want my cock inside that red pussy?"

"Yes, Captain."

"Why?" He bent forward on his hands to lean over me. Still not touching. Damn him. But he stopped close enough that I felt the heat from his naked body.

"Because"—I hissed in a breath as the clamp on my clit moved—"because you're the best."

"And?"

"The most fearsome pirate. Anyone would be—ah!—lucky to be with you."

"And?" His eyes had glazed and his hand crept toward the base of his shaft. I almost had him.

"And I love you, Captain. You're beautiful. You're everything that—"

He shoved ruthlessly into me, filling my sopping hole to the hilt.

For a moment, I couldn't speak.

"You're everything I want. Fuck you." My voice lowered. "Fuck me."

"Captain," he corrected, obeying anyway. He thrust in deep around my underwear, knocking the chain with every shove. The defined muscles of his arms bracketed my head.

He grunted and worked deep, rolling his body into mine.

His fingers tightened around the cushioned edge of the chair, flexing the trident.

I wanted a longer session, but I couldn't hold onto the thought. Desire erased everything else. The feel of him slipping thick and hard into me, the stimulation of the clamps on my breasts and clit, the sight of concentration and desire on his face as he fuck, fuck, fucked me. I hardly remembered who I was.

First a whimper, then a yell, then an outright scream ripped from my chest as I came. My legs straightened then shook like they were made of porridge.

Terion's bare hand, damp with water and sweat, rubbed up to my breast, hitting the tortuous clamp before removing it. His lips closed around the freed nipple. Saliva and tongue soothed it, and I was so far from caring about the spit rolling down my torso. He could suck me all night if he wanted to.

"No one does this like you, Captain," I said, breaking the rules and watching him as he strained. The view over his back and ass were enough to turn me on again.

"No one..." He groaned loudly. "No one feels like you. Terror."

With a surprised grunt, he arched back and pulsed into me, coming hard.

He collapsed forward in a kiss. I wanted to cup his head, but my hands were tied. He did it all, both hands cradling my face. His kiss took, nibbling and licking and stealing all it wanted.

I bit him back.

"You weren't submissive," he said hoarsely, reaching up to undo my bonds.

"Next time, you can force me to be."

"It's only because I'm tired."

My arms flopped down to my sides. "I suspected. Because you are Captain fucking Asterion, and I want all you can give me."

"You have to make it into a challenge," he muttered, helping me up. That involved freeing my sensitive clit. "My Mari."

As soon as I stood up, he took me in his arms. "My Terion," I murmured against his chest. My whole back was wet from the power that exploded from his hands when he came.

"You'll drive me mad."

"If madness means you'll punish me in this room, then..." I smirked suggestively.

He held me tighter against him. The body-length contact made my already wet center even slicker. I could go again.

"Insatiable," he teased.

"As the ocean."

A sound like a growl rumbled through his chest into mine. It resolved in a laugh. "That was a short one."

"But good," I finished.

He sighed contentedly. "Yes. I can do better."

"I know."

"What do you mean, you know?"

"Only you can make me scream."

"Mmmm. True. This body." He rotated with me in his arms. The movement let me feel some of his muscles. "You need it."

I wanted to say that arrogance was unattractive, but damn it, not on him. He'd earned it all. And I fucking loved it. "Fine."

His eyebrows rose. "Fine?"

"Fine, you can fuck me more often."

He laughed, hearty and suggestive. "Oh, I plan to."

"Good."

"Are you finally tired now, Mari?"

His face said that he would go for another round if I asked to begin again. "What does that new contraption do?" I cast my gaze at the new object on the wall.

"That? Experimental."

I didn't reply, waiting for him to elaborate.

"I enjoy nothing better than controlling your pleasure, Mari."

I nodded for him to go on.

"But if we ever wanted to experiment with a new arrangement..." He held up a finger in front of my face. "A rare arrangement. I'd be prepared for that."

My heartbeat quickened. I glanced again at the phallic object attached to straps and suddenly understood. "You'd let me lead? You'd let me fuck you?"

"In all the ways. I don't know if I'd like it, but..." He tipped his beautiful mouth.

I kissed him hard. What better challenge could there be than directing Captain Terion's pleasure? To have him squirm beneath my touch? To thrust into him and hear him whimper? I felt faint with anticipation. "We have to try it!"

"Now?" he asked after a too-long beat.

Against me, his dick felt only semi-hard and I felt tired after that trembling orgasm.

"No. Let's go to bed." I pressed my lips to his again, feeling down the length of his back. "What would happen if you left the coat here? Would Ajax melt?"

"He'd thank the gods."

"Then maybe we should give him a better show than last time."

"You know I need that jacket." He loved it. Leaving it out of easy reach wasn't something I really expected him to do.

"We could carry it?"

"You're wicked."

"The Terror."

He scooped me in, kissing the top of my head. "My Terror, thank the seas."

I tipped my face up to meet his. "I wouldn't want to run afoul of Captain Terion either."

"Gods help our enemies."

"To fall into our path," I finished.

He grinned, humming gladly. "You're the most wonderfully wicked thing I've ever brought on board." Sighing, he said, "All right, let's go to bed."

I kissed the scales on his face.

He slung the discarded jacket over one arm and offered me the other. "You can walk, I hope?"

I punched him lightly on the bicep. His cock still gleamed with traces of me.

Tomorrow. Unless we sailed into an emergency, we'd return tomorrow to try Terion's toe-curling, blood-heating suggestion that we temporarily switch roles. My thoughts swam through an ocean of possibilities. In this competition, we'd both win.

IF YOU LIKED THIS STORY, CHECK OUT *TEMPTATION AND TRIDENTS* (Terion and Mari's story) or any of the other Deathless Love books in the series. They're interconnected standalones, so you can begin wherever your mood or curiosity takes you!

❦ 3 ❦
DIRECTING THE FIVE

The goddess Ayame takes charge of the five males who love serving her needs.

This original story includes explicit sex, strong language, overstimulation, orgy, anonymity, voyeurism, light BDSM, MMMMMF, and DVP

One of my favorite places in the world was this shower. It rained over an entire corner of the room, whether by magic or clever construction, I didn't know.

The thought faded as Devotion crowded against me and hungrily pressed his lips to mine. His specialty was passion. I heard it in every word, felt it in every touch, tasted it in every kiss. His fingers traced my skin. A laugh bubbled up as my bare back touched the rock wall, warm with water.

"Ayame," he moaned, trailing kisses down my neck.

Only last week, the men hadn't known my name. I still didn't know theirs. We liked it that way. Devotion was, well, devoted, and the others fit their preferred names perfectly too.

I threaded my fingers through Devotion's thick black hair. Over his muscular, tan shoulder, I locked eyes with the leader, who sat by the door, watching. The intensity in his gaze took me by surprise. He wasn't as adoring as Devotion or as aggressive as Mace, but he had a magnetism I couldn't deny. His charisma could seduce anyone.

"Mace," the leader instructed.

All five males joined me today. Mace, like the rest, was naked. A scar bisected his eyebrow. At the word from the leader, he stalked under the water—no door or wall separated the shower from the rest of the room—and gripped my hair in a fist. Forcing my head toward him, he kissed me next. Mace didn't kiss with the soft insistence of a lover, but the need of someone who wanted to fuck. Now.

Sensation coated my body as Mace forced his tongue in my mouth and Devotion fell to his knees, kissing lower until the tip of my breast was in his mouth. Rain fell on my skin and the two stimulated me everywhere but the one place I wanted it most.

I whimpered. They were both erect as a wooden post, but not close enough to get inside me. "Please." I looked sideways at the leader again, whose dark eyes burned as he watched.

"She wants to be fucked," Mace growled against my mouth, pinching my cheeks together.

The leader only hummed.

Water from Mace's hair fell into my face and into my open mouth. I yearned. I *needed* more.

Reaching down, I felt for Mace's dick. As soon as my fingers brushed his shaft, he shoved Devotion away and stepped in front of me. "Don't do that unless..." he huffed, unable to finish the sentence. Half-lifting me, he speared inside my slippery pussy, faster and deeper than comfort.

I gasped.

He shook water out of his pale, angular face and gave an evil smirk, pinning me fully to the wall. Without more words, he pumped into me hard. Air gusted from my lungs every time his body slammed against mine. He was ruthless in a way I craved, an angry, desperate lover.

My cries pitched higher. His thrusts grew wilder. He gathered my thighs in his hands. I was weightless, held only by his body as it took what he wanted.

He slowed, piercing me with three more deep plunges as he exploded, filling me with his cum. His expression as he orgasmed was all gritted teeth and glazed eyes. I couldn't get enough.

"Mouth. Anchor." This from the leader again, whose voice had gone ragged at the edges. I loved how he orchestrated all our encounters, but one day I wanted to try leading. Maybe tomorrow.

Our sessions left me exhausted and sore, but I craved my males like I craved nothing else in life. I wanted their cocks, their tongues, their hands all over me. As soon as I left them, all I could think about was coming back.

Anchor, with his shaved head and enormous dick, approached with his lover Mouth, a smaller demi-god who could turn me into a quivering puddle with one flick of his expert tongue.

"Wait."

Everyone froze.

I inhaled slowly. "I want to lead."

The leader quirked a brow. "While we fuck you? Or you want to direct us with each other?" Even the leader had obeyed the will of clients before they met me. They enjoyed working together in this room behind the area designated for wild parties. Whoever wanted to pay could choose which of them to fuck, and they'd oblige. The first time I'd met them, I asked for all five. We'd barely been apart since.

I considered for a moment. "Both."

Mace, his chest still heaving, lowered a glare at me, but not a glare that meant he was angry. I knew them all well enough now that as I looked from face to handsome face, all but Mace hard as stone (and he was getting there again too), I could tell they were intrigued. Even eager.

Devotion gave the leader a pleading look.

"All right," said the leader, rising to approach, but not close enough to get under the rain shower. "What do you want us to do?"

Power zinged under my skin. Not only water but arousal dripped down my legs. The males all looked at me with excitement and appreciation.

How could I keep my head enough to coordinate everyone?

"I have an idea. All of us on the bed."

Beyond the shower there was a bed large enough for all six of us. They'd taken me here, separately or all together, many times. I needed more, more, more.

"Mouth, lie down."

Most of us were soaked from the shower, but nobody cared. Mouth flopped eagerly on his stomach, ready to suck me off.

"No, other way."

With a half-smile, he obeyed. I doubted he had a clue what I wanted him to do. Rather than riding that famous tongue, I had something new in mind. In all our trysts, Mouth had never fucked me with his cock. It was the smallest among the generous assortment here—something I appreciated when I gave him oral.

When I straddled him, they all looked a little surprised. He fit in easily, comfortably. He felt amazing. Different than Mace with his demanding thrusts or Anchor with his massive cock, but amazing all the same. Mouth's eyes widened, his lips parting in pleasure.

"Now Anchor," I said, not moving because I knew as soon as I did, my ability to organize anything would blow away like a puff of smoke. "Fuck his mouth like you want to."

Anchor's brows ticked downward. My heart galloped at my own boldness, but fuck it, we'd all done unspeakable things with each other. He couldn't really have been surprised by that idea.

Mouth reached for him. They linked hands before Anchor backed up. The position was a little awkward as Anchor bent forward over Mouth's face. Anchor's big ass got close to me as we both straddled the smaller demi-god.

"Devotion," I said next, ushering him forward. He leaned close to hear my instructions, so I whispered. "I want you in me too."

There were too many legs on the bed as Devotion hurried to do what I suggested. Because Mouth was a little smaller, I had room for another, and I knew Devotion loved to enter in multiples. So did I. It was overstimulating and painful and wonderful and everything.

I rose up on my knees to give him room to slide under and feed his stiff cock first through my folds to get wet and slippery, and then slowly, slowly, in next to the first. I shuddered as he went deeper, stretching me out.

Mouth made a gurgling noise. My attention had been so locked on Devotion that I hadn't seen Anchor stuff his massive shaft between Mouth's eager lips. Anchor's backside bobbed in front of me.

I reached out for something to hang on to—a body, a hand. The leader took my hand and laced his grip with mine. In his touch was a question. Was the setup complete? Would I try to fit anyone else in?

Struggling to think straight as Devotion gave slight pulses of his hips, I looked from the leader to Mace, who had already recovered from coming inside me a minute ago. He looked ready to devour me.

"You"—I squeezed the leader's hand—"kiss Devotion. I know you want to."

His answering expression wasn't easy to read. I released his hand and trailed my fingernail down his torso to his throbbing cock. "I'll do this while you do."

"Interesting." Our tangle of limbs grew as he settled himself down and cupped Devotion's face to kiss him. I encircled his length and pumped up and down, teasing him. Under me, Devotion's movement grew needier. I knew he'd enjoy making out with the leader. The idea of bringing in another person into the group bothered me, but I loved seeing my five enjoying each other. I didn't try to analyze it. Our arrangement was weird and erotic and didn't make much sense, but gods, we enjoyed each other. They addicted me, so I had no intention of stopping.

Beside the bed, Mace practically vibrated with tension.

"Mace, I need you to pinch me until I beg you to fuck my mouth."

When I began riding two cocks, bouncing and grinding as I went, the others made surprised noises that sounded like pleas. Anchor thrust into Mouth. When I looked behind me, Devotion, meeting my thrusts with his own, kissed the leader open-mouthed. His hand threaded through the leader's hair like I'd done to Devotion int he shower. In my hand, the leader's cock grew so heavy and hard that I struggled to make my fingertips meet around it.

A sharp pain twisted my head forward again. My nipple throbbed. Mace.

"You want me to fuck you again?" he taunted.

I bounced, streaming with shower water and new sweat, and nodded.

"Tell me." He grabbed my breast again so hard I knew it would leave bruises.

"Yes."

Anchor groaned. So did the leader. The smell of sex and sweat made my head swim.

"I need you to beg," hissed Mace between his teeth. His hand moved up to catch my jaw, forcing me to look up at him.

I liked that he was rough. I liked that Devotion was passionate, Anchor was huge, Mouth was talented, and the leader intentional. I had two cocks shoved deep inside me, thrusting for their own release, and I longed for more. My exes hadn't given me what I wanted: respect and insatiable sex. With these five, I had it all.

"Do it."

Mace pinched my other nipple, earning a yelp of pain. "I said beg."

"Do it. Fuck me. I need you inside me."

Apparently, that was enough. Mace stood on the bed and swung his leg over Anchor's moving form so he could shove his dick in my mouth. He held my head to his groin and thrust deep. I choked—I'd never had a strong gag reflex—and I fought to breathe around him. Saliva pooled in my mouth and coated his shaft.

Under me, Mouth and Devotion rolled their hips in uneven desperation. My hand on the leader's cock stopped its smooth rhythm, becoming jagged, because I couldn't think, couldn't fit anyone else in. I was choking, I was filled, I was so fucking turned on. My cries got lost around Mace's thick length. I ground so hard onto Mouth and Devotion that I thought I might bruise them too.

Anchor was first to break. I heard his loud groan, the telltale sign he was coming.

Mouth went next, his voice suddenly clear enough to hear too.

Devotion's cum joined Mouth's inside me. I was full and dripping and it still wasn't enough. My need was huge. It was monstrous. It demanded more.

The leader's cock twitched in my hand as he came all over the bed.

Finally, Mace shot his stream into my throat. I coughed, then swallowed.

I was so close myself that I rubbed at my clit to get myself there.

"No," said the leader, angling up on an elbow. "No." He moved my hand out of the way. Easing my leg to the side, he adjusted so he could lower his head between my thighs.

"Oooh!" My head fell back as the leader's tongue met my clit. It was like he'd learned from Mouth. He flicked over the exact spot I needed. Still filled by two cocks, I writhed, feeling them begin to harden again. His hands held me in place as he sucked me hard.

My mewls turned into something that sounded like sobs.

"That's it," said Devotion encouragingly.

I wasn't sure how, but they lifted and moved me so I lay on

my back. Devotion and Mouth were still inside. The leader's lips were still locked between my legs.

"Make her feel good," said someone. Anchor. I peeled my eyes open. Yes, Anchor. With this much stimulation, my ability to think clearly was gone.

Devotion thrust first. Mouth followed. They found a rhythm together, rolling their hips in unison and keeping the pace when I gasped and shivered.

"Make her shriek," said Mace from somewhere near my head.

No longer in sync, Devotion and Mouth braced themselves on the bed or on the leader who still sucked me off. They looked ridiculous—two beautiful, naked males riding me like a cantering horse.

The leader made a slight adjustment of his angle.

My back arched off the covers. The two dicks sawed into me more frantically. They hadn't needed any time to recover. It was like they felt as turned on as I did, with multiple breath-stealing orgasms barreling toward me. I whined, unable to stop myself.

There it was. The ache building, building...

Uncontrollable pleasure shook my limbs, erupting from my lips in a loud, strangled noise.

The air smelled musty. Devotion strained, poured into me again, gorgeous as a statue. Mouth's orgasm was less dramatic but no less messy.

"My gods," I croaked, slumping down.

My five settled around me.

I took a few moments to find more words. After that, I felt thirsty and my chest sweaty. I had to breathe.

"You." I tucked Devotion's har behind his ear and tried

again. "You have your specialties, but you didn't tell me you're multi-talented like this."

"That was amazing," Mouth groaned.

"Mm hm." Anchor touched Mouth's shoulder fondly.

"Are you glad I got to lead?" I raised a brow at the leader.

His unshakable confidence hadn't left, but something new I couldn't place layered on top of it as he looked back at me. "You've given me ideas."

I didn't hold back the smile that spread over my face. "Give me an hour, then I'm ready when you are."

IF YOU LIKED THIS STORY, CHECK OUT MORE ABOUT AYAME and her five in *Lovers and Monsters*!

4
WRITING THE STRANGER

After decades of anonymous letter writing, it's finally time to meet.

This original story includes explicit sex, strong language, parental abuse, mention of murder, mention of sexual abuse and trafficking, isolation, masturbation, and a tail

80 years ago

Seawater splashed around my ankles. Gray clouds streaked the wet sky, threatening rain. I curled my lip, wading onward.

I'd noticed the rock formation when I was a child playing on the beach. Brown and porous, the rock rose out of the Corae Sea like a huge piece of coral. For some reason, it called to me.

To get to it, I had to cross to the far end of beach, past the boundary of my mother's province, and wade out during low tide.

Today seemed as good a day as any to see it up close. My mother, goddess of sapphires, ruled this corner of the island, one too small even to be absorbed by one of the Eight Realms. Rulers had fought over it throughout the centuries, but eventually they forgot about us and my mother took up ruling again. I didn't know who my father was, though my mother ought to have remembered. It was only twenty years ago.

She should have cared, but she didn't. Not about my unnamed father and certainly not about me.

My eyes stung as I reached the rocks, placing my palm against their rough surface. I'd seen this place enough times that I could have walked through the air, like all deathless could do, disappearing in one place and appearing here, but I wanted to feel the burn of my thighs as water resisted my approach. I needed something, anything, to ground me. Besides, traveling through the air left residue that would make it easier for her to find me.

Would I make sure our visitors felt "comfortable"? That was what she asked. At first, I hadn't understood what she meant. When servants furtively left a sheer outfit in my room, my throat filled with panic. I didn't know any of the deathless people due to arrive soon to marvel at the sapphire-studded palace. But what Mother asked, Mother got. Her requests were commands. It was up to the listener to interpret and do, or else feel her wrath.

I didn't want to obey, but what choice did I have? I had nowhere else to go. Mother's power on this side of the island was absolute. And Kohi was remote enough that I didn't have anyone else to turn to—no aunts or grandmothers, friends or even a father who might help. I couldn't travel through the air at random because we were surrounded by the sea. I couldn't picture a location for escape, and if I landed in the water, I wouldn't be able to jump again. I was a demi-goddess with the power to hold my breath for hours, but I could still drown.

I weighed my options. Maybe it would be better to drown than to do as Mother asked. Her image and reputation as a wealthy and powerful goddess meant far more than the offspring of a quick human fling.

My body was my own, wasn't it? But Mother owned that too, apparently able to sell me as easily as a cut of meat.

Making visitors comfortable didn't mean drawing baths. Servants did that. She wanted me to warm their beds and perform whatever acts the temple courtesans did. I didn't even know what those acts were. Knowing rudimentary anatomy helped me imagine what they might ask me to do. But I didn't want to. I didn't want to.

What I wanted was a confidante. If I suffered like this, I wanted someone else to know. But there was no one to tell but the sea.

I'd spent all night writing down my woes, all the hatred and fear and embarrassment I felt, in a rambling letter to no one. Getting the words out helped a little. I stopped crying.

A bitter laugh puffed out my nose as I gripped the stoppered bottle with the pages inside. This child's idea wouldn't solve anything. Still, giving my words to the sea loosened my tightly clenched heart.

Maybe one day, someone would read the anonymous note and feel passing sadness for me. We'd be bound across time in that moment. The notion was almost romantic.

One of the holes in the rock looked the right size. Yes, the circular end fit perfectly, with the stoppered end barely visible as it stuck out.

I sighed.

A stranger might find out my fate. Even if they didn't, the sea and the rocks and the sky witness about the injustice of keeping me trapped here like a pet. Growing up didn't diminish the danger, but enhanced it. Mother could exploit me in new ways. I dreaded to discover what she'd think of next.

Casting one last look at the bottle tucked into the rock formation, I turned away. It started to rain.

75 years ago

It wasn't just one thing this time. It was the daily slog of being dismissed and forgotten until I was convenient. It was the neglect.

Honestly, this morning, it was the egg. When I went down to breakfast, one egg in a jeweled cup waited for me. Eggs made me sick. Mother had known that for years and yet this was the second day in a row that she'd ordered the same breakfast for me as for herself. Nothing about me mattered enough to remember. I tracked down a raw piece of fruit and retired to my room to pen a new letter to no one. After leaving the first one, I hadn't really expected to return, but layers of resentment and desperation had risen high enough that I needed release again. My blood raced as I wrote, one eye on the door.

To the sea, it said. *Nothing has changed. Mother sees me as a tool, not a person. When I'm not useful, she ignores me. I asked to leave the island last month. She laughed, but I saw the murder in her eyes. Is it really better to live here than to run away? I know the answer. Mother can find me anywhere. She'd destroy anyone who helped me. I can't get out.*

You are my sea. Tomorrow, I'll take a good, long swim.

I hate my mother. I said it. It's written down, so I'll take this to the rock. That way a servant won't find it in my room. I wish someone would save me. I wish I could save myself.

I left it unsigned.

The sharp smell of ocean washed over me as I waded to the brown sea rock where I'd slotted my letter into a hole five years ago. There was the cork of the glass bottle, barely visible.

And was that... another bottle?

Irritation threaded with fear surged up. Another bottle meant one of three things—someone else used my spot to leave their own notes, which felt like a violation. I didn't own the rock, but it still felt like one of the only things that was truly mine. Private and important. Or, a worse option, Mother had discovered my secrets. The idea left my belly cold. What would she do if she knew I confided my real feelings in notes like this? Why hadn't she punished me for it already?

That last idea gave me a small amount of comfort. She would have. I'd said such personal things in that letter. It was long and rambling, detailing the pain she'd caused me, my resentment, the way she'd twisted something I'd secretly desired into a dirty and horrible thing when she'd offered me to those guests.

Then there was the third option: a reply. It felt like a distant possibility, but then, there was the new bottle, its cork encrusted with salt.

In the five years since I'd tucked my first note into the rock, I hadn't found a friend to talk to about any of this. If I did find one, I doubted I could dredge up this much honesty out loud. On the mere suspicion of insulting her, Mother had tortured servants who were kind to me. I wasn't sure exactly what she did to them, but I heard them screaming from other parts of the palace. Sickness rose up my throat at the memory.

Maybe I shouldn't have written down anything. If Mother discovered that I really did resent her, that my discontent had found words, she'd punish not only me but whoever had replied.

I approached the new bottle. The cork was plain, like mine, but cleaner, newer. Hands trembling, I rubbed crystals of salt from the rim with my thumb. No symbol indicating a particular god or goddess. Heart pulsing in my throat, I drew it out of the rock. A rolled-up piece of paper lay inside. Swallowing hard, I thumbed off the cork and rolled the paper onto my finger so it became tight enough to fit through the top. Balancing my own note and this mystery became awkward, so I carefully placed my short letter into a hole closer to the bottom. Clustering them together might look suspicious from a distance. Others, apparently, knew about this rock, and I didn't want to draw more attention.

Taking the ends of the mystery note between my fingers, I unrolled it. The script was larger than mine, but neat. What I'd thought was a short note was actually very thin sheets folded together.

No one should feel this alone, so I'm leaving this here to say that I am willing to listen to anything you can't speak aloud. I won't tell anyone, so secrets are safe with me. To prove it, you don't even need to tell me who you are. I'm content with staying anonymous. The truth is, I need a listening ear as well sometimes. This seems like a good solution to me. This way, we can know, no matter what is happening to us, that someone somewhere cares.

If you see this, I want you to know that I hate your mother also. No daughter should endure what you have endured. I don't even know you, yet I've seen the way you think clearly and empathetically simply through your writing. She is blind if she doesn't recognize you as more than means for a bribe.

Write again.

So you have a piece of me and know you don't have to fear what I'll say, here's something. I'm a demi-god (all I'll say about my identity) but I can't see. I can see close up but nothing far away, which worries me. Someday, I think a rival or enemy will find out this fact and use it to kill me. Now we each have a protected secret.

Your secret friend

I stared at the letter long after I'd finished reading it. My throat swelled with longing. I was a storm, all my waves heaving and chaotic.

This wasn't like Mother's attempt at amends, when she'd stroke my hair and tell me she believed I could do better after all, that we could visit my favorite place on the cliffs. This felt different. Soothing. The writer didn't ask for money or favors beyond an honest reply.

After reading the note again to memorize what I could, I carefully rolled up the paper and fed it into the bottle. Thank the Divine I'd kept my hands dry, despite being knee-deep in water.

There was no doubt this stranger meant the letter for me. I wanted to shove it in my pocket and take it home, but that meant risking discovery. That wasn't an option. A pull like yearning connected me to the writer of this letter.

After placing my new note beside the kind stranger's, my fingertips lingered on the top of the bottle. Did it matter that I'd opened it? Would someone notice the fingerprints on the glass and the angle of the cork? Did it matter?

My gaze fell on the note I'd brought. Knowing that someone had opened the first bottle changed how I felt about it. I wanted to read it through again, to make sure it didn't sound whiny or entitled. What if the stranger read the new letter too?

I left the first five years ago. He—if it was a he—could have seen it any time between then and now.

Twice, I realized. He must have come here twice. Once to see my letter and once to drop off his own.

Something like fear crawled in my belly. I didn't want a stranger finding me here, even this stranger who seemed kind. Hadn't my letter said something about wishing someone would rescue me? I cringed, then lifted my chin. I would have written the letter either way. I had no choice. Either I wrote my feelings down, or I screamed into my pillow until I was hoarse.

Whiny. Entitled. Words my mother used to describe me all the time. Maybe she was right.

With one final look at the mysterious extra bottle, I turned to wade back to my life.

STELLA PURRED IN MY LAP AS I STROKED HER BACK. SHE LAY on my legs while I stretched out on my bed, thinking. I'd read for a few minutes, but I couldn't focus. Spoiling Stella helped me relax enough to think clearly.

Long cat hair stuck to my palm. Every few strokes, I scraped the hair off into a wastebasket. Already, a cloud of light gray was forming at the bottom of the metal basket.

Mother hadn't committed some new sin that compelled me to write. Everything had been normal for a while. My life wasn't a romp filled with adventure or romance that people liked to read about. But I wanted to write another letter, a longer one this time.

At the very least, I needed to return to the rock soon to see if my latest letter had been opened.

He could be dangerous.

I scraped off my palm and went back to petting Stella. The cat stared absently, eyes half-closed, at the opposite wall of my bedroom. Nothing over there but a tall, bronze looking-glass that appeared in my room when I was a child, and a painted screen, folded and leaning against the wall. I rarely used it because people never visited my room.

I chewed on the words in the stranger's letter as if they were food, savory and life-sustaining. If they contained hidden poison, I couldn't taste it. He didn't seem dangerous. It seemed like he wanted to be friends. What a ridiculous thing to have to puzzle out by myself...

Because I could never tell Mother. Even the servants were warned not to speak to me. Mother said it was about rank and respect. I would have welcomed conversation with the servants anyway, but they feared Mother too much to disobey.

The letter writer should too. Danger surrounded him, whether he was a target or contributor. Even though my body throbbed with the desire to run, run away to him now, I couldn't. Mother needed me to make more money, and she would find us. When she did, everything and everyone we'd ever cared about would be in danger. The very idea of escape was selfish. Mother was right about me—I was self-centered and unwilling to put my desires aside for the good of others. My eyes felt hot.

Abruptly, Stella stood and walked away. I scraped the cat hair off my hand, picked through the blanket where she'd lain for the rest of the fluffs I could see, and went to fetch a new bottle to bring to the sea rock.

To you,

 I found your letter. Maybe you left it years ago, but I needed to say thank you.

 These bottle messages make me sound more interesting and mysterious than I feel. Most of my days are mundane. I go swimming sometimes. I have a cat. My life is small and directed.

 I can hold my breath for hours. I'm deathless too. Compared to your letter, this one already sounds unimpressive, but in case you read these, I wanted to tell you that finding your note felt like the first breath of air after hours. If you don't want to be friends with a stranger, I understand. We can't meet, but I would be happy to write for as long as you want.

 Yesterday, I caught a sprite looking in the dining room window. I shooed it away because Mother would have grown enraged if she saw another one there. When she was young, who knows how long ago, a sprite sent her a three-day vision of her own death, and she's never forgiven them. She can't die. She's a full goddess. That's the most interesting thing that I can think of that's happened lately. At least, since the last party she had in the spring, but I don't want to talk about that. I like it when it's quiet. The best would be if she had one well-behaved guest. That way, they would have all her attention and I could slip away with my cat or the waves and not be a bother. I hope your life has a little more color in it. Even if I don't hear back from you, I'll cherish your letter.

To my friend,

I didn't think you'd find my reply. I hoped you would. Imagine how surprised I was to find two new messages!

Why don't you swim away if you can hold your breath that long? Or travel through the air? It sounds like you're still unhappy. Lately, life here (I don't live near the rock, but I visit regularly) has been chaotic. I don't suggest you flee to my home, if you were thinking it.

Tell me more about your cat. Feral cats, and one I suspect is a demigoddess, absolutely infest the hills near the home of one of my brothers. I enjoy seeing him annoyed.

I will look for your reply next time I visit here, which is always during the first low tide.

VISITING THE ROCK BECAME A WEEKLY ESSENTIAL. MOST weeks came with a note from the stranger. I sucked up his messages like air. We talked about Stella and the foods we liked, the deities we'd met and whether we liked them. I learned he had a tail. I told him I was more beautiful than I was. When Mother wronged me, I told him. When I wondered about humans and death, I told him. Secrets I held close came out piece by piece. And in no time at all, I felt like I was falling in love.

70 years ago

I floated underwater, no longer swimming. Here, the waves were gentle, sound muted, everything blue and hazy. Lumpy gray barnacle fish and fire-bright lightning eels zigzagged the sea bed below. Waving my arms and legs slowly, I managed to stay suspended.

Mother acted suspicious. I went to the rock every few days to leave another message for my stranger and to read his response. It was too often to go unnoticed, but I couldn't help it. I yearned for him.

Between funny stories and frustrations we both had at home, he'd write piercingly romantic things that made my eyes well.

Yesterday, I'd recited the words to myself on the way to another guest's room. *You are as vast as a purple sky to me. We have purple sunsets here in the winter. They stretch on and on with orange clouds. I have two paintings of them in my room because one wasn't enough. I needed a new angle of this beauty I couldn't see. I'm looking at one now and my chest aches for more of it. It aches for you. I ache for you.*

I ached for him too, but I had to stuff his words deep down into the most secret part of me to fulfill my duty for the guest. I'd bathed twice and now, this morning, I swam. To me, the stranger wasn't like the sunset. He was like the ocean. His anonymity made him infinite, but the minute details of his life made him real.

My stomach lurched as I imagined us finally meeting—an impossible thing, since Mother would kill me and probably him too. The stranger would approach and touch me between my legs, there, rubbing and caressing until all my reality stopped existing and it was only us there. Our pleasure would be everything in life.

Bubbles passed my lips as I grunted, still holding my breath, finding the slick spot that made my desire crest and toes curl. No spy would find me here. I could indulge the fantasy.

What if he took his time with me instead of jumping right in? What if he cared about my pleasure as much as his? What if he kissed me the way I longed for? What if he asked first?

50 years ago

I didn't want to meet the stranger. At this point, destroying the mystery would mean destroying one of the only good things in my life. Writing to him felt more like writing in a diary than writing to a lover. He was more than a lover to me. He was an extension of myself.

To you,

I hope Sarpa has recovered from her fever. Although I like having my bed to myself, I imagine that you want her back and feeling well again.

Mother took me to Nalia last week. I've heard about beautiful places in Nalia, but she took us to a small city on the coast that was crowded and smelled like fish. Based on what I saw, they must read the walls instead of books, because everything from names to costs and accounts were posted there. She's trying to prove that she isn't a monster. I know that's why she took me there. She even bought me a nice dinner, but she still ordered for me. I wouldn't have chosen the fish and vegetables, but the seasoning tasted good. The city was called Pelatinos. Have you been there?

To my friend,

Sarpa is gathering rain water because she says it tastes better than the water we usually drink. She asked about you. Even though I've explained, as much as I can, about you, she doesn't believe me. I hope she does soon. I won't give up these letters and I don't want to give up Sarpa either. It's difficult to understand for her, I'm sure. I would be confused in her place.

For the appearance tonight, even though I'm one of the lesser deathless in attendance, I think I'll wear the dark gray and green ceremonial outfit. What do you think? I could choose the blood-red one instead, but no, I wouldn't change my mind even if you thought I should wear the dark red. Gray is better for this. It's serious but not aggressive, since I'm advocating for peace. My presence won't be the one that matters, but to say more would give you too many hints about me. I will, of course, tell you how the meeting goes.

40 years ago

My stranger asked again why I couldn't leave. It struck me as an odd question. I had detailed what I now understood were violent abuses that my mother had inflicted on me and the servants. I couldn't risk him. Then, a horrifying idea surfaced.

Thousands of letters later, I looked at my mother and wondered, at last, if she was behind them all.

She emerged on the stone and sapphire terrace where I'd been writing a new letter. Immediately, her gaze fell on me, blue eyes icy. Lazy, that meant. Worthless.

I covered up the paper with my arm. Her stunning dress reminded me—I was supposed to change for the visit from the minor Zenian goddess and her family. For hours, I'd stood while the tailor fussed over the intricate pattern that Mother insisted I wear. It was a dress with removable panels, already sensual, blue of course, and erotic when taken to pieces. Our visitors included three male demi-gods she expected to be interested in my services.

Years of practice had dulled my emotions about any of it. But when Mother looked toward the paper under my arm, a bolt sparked through me.

A stranger.

A demi-god.

The person I spilled every secret to.

Mother could find no worse way to hurt me than waiting decades to reveal that I'd never found hope after all. Maybe she wanted me to look at every visitor and wonder if it was my stranger.

For a while I burned so passionately for him that I tried to run away. My thoughts circled around him like birds over prey. Every night, I moaned in desperation, touching myself and imagining it was my stranger.

Now, it had become more than that. I felt like I was talking to myself whenever I wrote, every word honest and raw and fearless. My stranger would always be a mystery, but whoever it was now knitted to my soul. He was there when I befriended a servant. We grew close for four years. When Mother found out I had a new confidante, she had my friend killed. Painfully.

If Mother wrote these letters, the last piece of my spirit would die.

"Why are you never helping?" Mother demanded, cold and regal as a gem.

"I... will now." Folding my letter small so it could fit in my hand, I followed her back inside.

To you,

What proof can you give me that you're real? I can't leave or meet you.

To my friend,

Did I do something to make you think I'm not who I say I am? Who else would spend forty years telling you everything? You know that I sweat when I eat melonberry, that Sarpa and I ended our relationship because I lied to her about you, that "When the Clouds Fall" is the only song from the spring festival that I don't hate, that my mother was a sacrifice to my monster father, and that I like to have sex from behind because I can go deeper that way. Who in this world would lie to you about all that? You know me like I know myself. As much as I would love to take you away, I know better than to beg. I don't know what more I could do to prove myself.

20 years ago

Every night I wrote to him. It was like talking to myself. Getting the words out of my mind and onto paper let me breathe again.

5 years ago

To you,
I can't stand it. An eternity alone isn't worth living. I'll do something drastic.

Now

I killed my mother.

To you,

The trial is in two days. I have two days of freedom, and I choose to spend them with you. I want to finally see your face. Come get me by the rock. Bring me home.

I rolled my shoulders before placing the new bottle among a hundred others that crowded into grooves of the jagged brown rock like barnacles. My breaths came shallow. It took everything in me to take a step, a breath. Existence paused. If I kept myself stiff and still and quiet, nothing would make me fall apart.

I'd killed my mother.

Well, she was a goddess, so she couldn't be killed, not really. The chest I'd buried under the house contained pieces of her, but she'd return and when she did...

That time was far off, and yet the idea frightened me more than the prospect of the god-prison Abaddon. The trial would determine if I went there, consigned to torture among the worst immortals who ever existed. I wouldn't last long.

Now that Mother wasn't here—I'd done the worst already, so what more could she say if she were?—I had to meet my stranger. I'd taken pains never to find him at the rock. The pull to go with him would have broken me. But now I had two days, one night before my reckoning.

I wanted some joy before the end. The stranger was friend, lover, confidante, myself. We were one. Eighty years of everyday thoughts and obsessions and joys and pain all documented to one another. It would have been simple, maybe, to determine his identity if I'd been allowed more movement around the island. I knew he wasn't from here, but traveled through the air to reach the sea, my sea. Because I couldn't talk to anyone, I never found out exactly who he was.

Today I'd find out.

Drawing in a salt-scented breath, I counted the waves. Holding air in my lungs like this felt almost like a trance. I'd done it regularly for years to calm down, recenter myself.

He's coming to get you.

He already knew everything about me. We had no need for introductions or small talk. I saw a tiny splash on the page in his letter to me after my first cat had died. He had a full inventory of everything to do with me and mine.

Sunlight glittered on the gentle waves. Maybe it was better this way. Mother gone. The stranger about to arrive.

I'd reached my breaking point and hardly recognized myself as I attacked. My entire being was no.

The stranger hadn't responded to my final letter, but he didn't need to. I'd know him from a gesture in a crowded room, even though we hadn't met. He was none of the faceless demi-gods with gaudy rings and stiff cocks. I knew that as surely as I knew he'd come to take me away and make me forget everything but him for two blissful days.

For the first time since I was young (I still looked young) my stomach dropped not from dread, but from genuine excitement.

A light splash made me open my eyes.

There he was. I knew him instantly. He was a barely adjusted version of the picture in my mind. From the golden hair to the dark, deep-set eyes narrowed at me, the height and build, and finally the tail like a lion waving behind him.

I hurried toward him, soaking in the nuance that messages couldn't capture. He was real and he was here.

"My friend," he said. It was his voice, his real voice.

Thickness made it hard to swallow. "It's you."

We met in calf-deep water. Instantly, our foreheads touched, our arms wrapped around each other. I breathed in his nearness. He was warm and his skin smelled like dust and citrus. His fingers curled into the damp fabric of my shirt.

After thousands of words, we didn't need them now. Even without names, I trusted him more than anyone in this world. My future hung suspended, like a fruit about to fall. Held like this, not grasping but steady, it felt like he had caught me.

His lips met the crown of my bowed head. The loneliness of all those days, weeks, years flooded me in a rush, and I leaned against his neck, trying not to sob. He was around my height, like we'd been paired somehow at birth. The extremes I'd endured lately had apparently made me poetic.

Darkness squeezed around us, tightening, tightening. He lived farther away than I had guessed. Finally, the sensation stopped. I inhaled deeply and looked around.

We stood in a room with a window overlooking the sea. It was similar to my sea, but the colors didn't quite match what I was used to. He was right that the sky looked purple. The smell coming through his window was less fishy and more floral. The sun was setting. Inside the room, the walls were papered with illustrations of sunsets.

"That's mine!" I pointed to one at eye level. After he'd said he couldn't see sunsets well himself, I'd painted him one and sent it with my letter. It wasn't good—three bars of color over blue water, with a white half-circle sun disappearing in the waves. That was toward the beginning of our correspondence. "You still have it?"

When I turned, he was half-smiling at me. "Of course."

That shouldn't have surprised me. I knew layers of his life that even his close friends didn't know.

The rest of the room was larger than mine, with a large bed dominating the side away from the window, a desk and oddments on the other side. Oars and tall metal lobster traps, chests and stacks of pillows and books. He'd done a lot of research about his mysterious family only to discover that his mother had been a human sacrifice to a monstrous demi-god. His tragedy had made him more compassionate. It didn't make him kill anyone.

I had two days.

As if the weather knew my struggle, a cloud moved over the sun streaming into the room.

"Our clothes are wet," he said.

"We usually change clothes after sending messages."

His expression said he remembered too.

It was so strange going from living with a mother who barely remembered a thing about me, even though I'd seen her almost every day of my life, to meeting someone for the first time who felt like the lost piece of my soul. He remembered everything.

When I thought I was in love with him—that feeling came and went in waves over the decades—I told him my most intimate secrets, the way they changed as time passed, the most outlandish desires that one day I hoped to fulfill.

The numbness I felt in the ocean turned to confidence now, something settled. I approached him, heartbeat quickening.

His hands rose at the same time mine did. Fingertips brushing my collar, he gently seized the first button. This was nothing like my experiences before—so foreign that it felt utterly new. My second thought was how I would describe this to my stranger. But I didn't have to. Now, our conversation was words, punctuation, and silence made of hands.

As he worked the buttons of my shirt through the holes, one by one, I unlaced the front of his top. It crisscrossed down his chest, covering an undershirt beneath. This was the cool season, but I couldn't help wondering if he felt hot and that was why his neck and jaw flushed red.

His words to me flashed through my mind.

I ache for you. Was that still true?

I never doubted that he would come for me if I asked. Wasn't that love?

I leaned into the breeze-light touch of fabric against my collarbone, my sternum. It whispered against my breasts as he peeled apart my layers. My breathing sounded loud in the silence, even though I knew it was only a shallow rush of air through my nose.

He was familiar and strange and, at that moment, everything I'd ever longed for wrapped in one suspended moment.

I reached the end of the laces, but he took his time, shrugging off the vest and moving closer to me in the same motion. His fingers never left my shirt.

Everyone just takes, I'd written once. *They don't wonder about me. I'm an object, and they pounce.*

Everything my stranger did was deliberate and slow. Instead of ripping off my clothes and making demands, he savored every new view of skin that peeked beneath my clothes. My yearning pierced so high I nearly moaned. His fingertips brushing between my breasts, almost too light to feel, made me wetter than grasping sexual encounters had.

Stomach balled tight, I curled my hands around the bottom of his flowing, cream-colored undershirt and raised it above his head. Smooth skin fuzzed with chest hair covered ridges of muscle. I loved that his body looked lived in, loved, used. Unlike some I'd been forced to entertain, he didn't have each muscle tightly defined on his abdomen. Instead, the muscles showed up when he moved.

When he bent closer to me. On the final buttons now, his hands paused, pulling down to tighten the fabric on the back of my neck. Not resisting, I leaned forward. Our lips met. His were soft, passionate. I met him with the same quiet intensity.

But our kiss didn't last long. We both knew there would be more time to taste each other, open-mouthed. As he pushed the final button through its hole, he gave a small, private smile. He liked to be undressed during moments like this. Our intimate knowledge of each other made it unfair for any other partner.

He stripped my shirt off, exposing me to him. His hot chest met mine. With a rasp, my shirt fell to the floor and he kissed me deeper this time, tracing my jaw, moving his hands through my hair. His air became my air. His body was like mine. We moved together.

I found the tail at the base of his spine. His pants, modified to button up around it, came off. I smoothed my hand over the expanse of his back and down to the thick tail waving behind him. It was furred and tufted, like a lion's. For years I'd known about his demi-god feature, but feeling it beneath my palm was completely different. As I stroked it up and down, with and against the short hair growing on it, it felt like it was mine. The stranger's kisses grew more insistent, almost as if I could control the intensity with my movements.

He pulled down my skirt and there we were, bare, body to body. Every breath into my mouth, every nibble of my lip, left me slick and needy. I nodded against him.

Drawing even closer, he picked me up in strong arms and brought me to the bed. His hard cock teased my clit as he held me close. Before, stimulation like that (if it happened at all) was accidental, but he'd done that on purpose. I wanted more. I *needed* more.

Had I asked him to make me forget? We talked long ago about what it would feel like to have him inside me, for my walls to squeeze around him, for him to rub my clit, and for me to drench his dick in my cum. Apparently, I didn't need to ask for intimacy over these two days. My stranger understood what I needed. He wanted the same.

We fell on the bed, him on top. We lined up perfectly. Back cushioned by soft blankets, I widened my legs to invite him inside. He reached down. His eyes glazed when he felt how slick I was and pushed the head in.

Neck already getting sweaty, I bit back a cry as he pressed deeper. Deeper. I was warm and wet and open and he filled me even more.

I croaked with need and surprise at how big he was, how good he felt. My hands flew to my mouth. I couldn't be loud.

His body stilled above me, and he gently removed my

hands from my lips. He searched my face wonderingly for a moment before he said, "No need to be quiet anymore."

Wasn't everybody quiet when they did this? To be loud was to bother. To be obvious was to become a target.

My heart and mind raced. I inhaled a long, deep breath. "You're right." I'd never considered that silence might have been another rope my mother had tied around me.

He kissed my hot cheek. "You're free." Lowering to whisper warm in my ear, he added, "You can make any sound you want."

As if daring me to take him up on that, he pulled out and thrust slowly all the way in again.

Only a jagged breath forced its way between my lips.

His pace increased, the movements growing sharper. I held onto him as he bucked.

Suddenly, he pulled out, leaving me empty.

"What?" I began, feeling tousled and disoriented.

But he was on his knees on the side of the bed, bringing his face between my thighs.

I clasped my hand over my mouth, then tore it away, as he licked my dripping sex. Not just licked, but flicked his tongue, explored, latched onto my clit in an explosion of white sparks.

I refused to stop my moan as he sucked that spot that craved friction. Soon, I thrust against his mouth, no sense of where I was or what I was doing. Madness claimed me and webbed across my skin. My groans climbed to a higher pitch as my body teetered on the edge of control. The blankets in my fists felt damp with sweat.

"Oh... oh my gods!"

With a final thrust, I seized and shuddered—he didn't let go—and I came hard into his mouth.

I'd come before, but never remotely like *that*.

"Oh!" I breathed as he climbed on top of me again. I'd forgotten to watch his face as he sucked me. I'd remember next time.

"Good?" His dancing eyes already knew the answer.

I nodded.

When he kissed me, I tasted myself. I'd found release, but the madness hadn't shaken off. Instead, craving grew to a roar.

We moved to the middle of the bed. When he sat up and scooped me to straddle his lap, I was already reaching for his length. I needed him in me, around me, a part of me. In this position, we could thrust into each other—not one or the other, but both. My lips curled at the edges as I got to work grinding against him, chasing release for us both. Friction friction friction. His hands cupping my ass, my hand in his hair, the other around his back, the grunts as we both reached for more, his tail wrapping around me, holding me like another arm.

I quivered. After my orgasm, this felt different. The sweetness from before still lingered like an aftertaste, but we were serious now. I wanted to wring all the pleasure I could from him, and he forced pleasure out of me. It was as if a storm had brewed across the water while I hadn't noticed. Now it was here, clouds dark as night, lightning about to crack the sky open.

No more waiting. We had now, so I would take it like I'd finally taken my life into my own hands.

I ground hard into his lap. He felt the shift too. I could tell because his tail pressed harder into my back, his mouth fell open in concentration, and his nails pinched my skin.

This was good, but it wasn't enough.

"Take me. Take me!" I ordered, feeling wild. I didn't tell

males what to do. But my stranger wasn't any of them. He was mine. We were each other's. We shared a soul.

I leapt off his lap onto the bed. Regretting the instant of separation, I got on hands and knees.

He chuckled with anticipation. In seconds, he positioned himself behind me, anchored his hands on my hips, and slid in. All the way in. Loosened from earlier, I didn't need to make room. The test seemed to be for himself. How deep could he go? Seated to the hilt, he ratcheted his hips back and slammed in, harder than before.

I hinged forward, gripping the bedsheets on either side of my head, now pressed against the blankets.

He thrust hard and fast, slapping against me every time, growling as his movements grew desperate. "Oh, fuck!" he gritted out. "Ah, fuck!"

Barely in control anymore, a creature of need, he fumbled forward, hand blindly feeling between my legs. I yelled when he parted my lips and found my clit again. An excited breath from him said he wanted me messy and desperate as he was. His thumb rubbed. His hard cock pumped in hard.

I writhed and couldn't find relief. I might have been begging or sobbing or I didn't know what. All I knew was his heat.

The lightning gathered, glowed, and bolted down in a rib-shaking crack. His efforts made us come together with loud, high noises and heavy spurts of cum.

When he pulled out of me, warm liquid trailed down the back of my thigh. I breathed hard, sweaty hair matted around my face.

The mattress shifted. My stranger had moved. I sat up. He sat on the edge of the bed, reaching for drawer. Inside was a cloth.

Returning to me, he sighed. "It's been a long time," he said with a drowsy smile.

He didn't mean since he'd last had sex. He meant the long time we'd waited to meet. By habit, my body readied itself for the other half of that thought—that it was my fault we hadn't met. If we'd met sooner, maybe all those bad things wouldn't have happened to me.

He said none of that. He didn't even imply it in the way he looked at me.

Instead, he cleaned me with the cloth, finger combed my hair, and brought me something to eat and drink. By the time he returned to bed with water, wine, and a spiced loaf of bread, I was so moved that I took the tray from him, set it out of the way, and hugged him. We still hadn't dressed yet. As he wrapped his arms and then his tail around me, the moment didn't feel sexual. It was a layer deeper. My stranger hadn't saved me by whisking me away to his bedroom when I asked. He'd saved me by becoming my friend.

"You don't need to go back for the trial," he said, at the same time I thought it.

"We need to get rid of the messages."

"We'll bring them." He sipped his wine.

Traveling through the air, as we could, left a residual trail that some people could sense. "We need to do it today."

I had no time to feel guilty. I didn't feel guilty. Mother had made my life an unbearable prison, and my stranger didn't have anyone in his life who knew him better than me. Besides, he could visit his home as long as I never visited mine.

We lingered in bed a while longer. Just before sunset, we gathered up decades of messages in little bottles—some needed to be pried out of the sea rock—unpinned my amateur painting to take with us, and left together.

I couldn't see the life ahead of us, and neither could he, but I knew I felt absolutely right in his arms. On the horizon glowed a glorious, multi-colored sunset that gilded the clouds. One long, stormy day was ending, and another was ready to begin.

5
LURING A SACRIFICE

When her followers lure a male into her sanctum, Aber finds him more tempting than anyone who's come before.

This original story includes explicit sex, strong language, mention of cannibalism, mention of blood, anonymity, and the implication of orgy

No one appreciated the geometry of tide pools: the interconnected webs and straight reeds, the magically logical tangle of it all.

I was in no mood to frolic through the mazes leading out of the porous cave system to the outside world. Today had been a dark day. It was a day that called for cups of rimbar.

Lwa leaned toward me, refilling my cup. Her dark, graceful fingers caressed the pitcher as if it were a lover. "What do you require today?" she crooned.

I drew a finger under her chin. "I require nothing."

"A new section to the maze? We would love new paths."

Another of my followers nodded from across the domed area.

I swished bare toes through the tide pool at my feet. Being connected to the geometry and intricacies of the natural world soothed me.

The truth was, I was hungry. But I couldn't allow my suna to grab just anyone to sate my hunger. Crabs would have to be enough again. Beneath my skin, restlessness itched. I needed, I needed, I needed.

This violent energy propelling me even in quiet moments had drawn many of my followers to me. They were all female, all beautiful in their ways. They wanted a new kind of savagery, one that didn't create victims but reveled in freedom. I'd always been singular, obsessive, thirsting for flesh. On quieter days like this one, I wondered if I was everything my suna craved. Maybe I was simply a weird demi-goddess pondering the geometry of reeds in a cave.

I met Lwa's eyes. "I'll consider the maze, my child."

She was no child. A human from Nalia, she had so much life to live, and she chose to spend it twirling in my mazes, luring people toward me for no reward but my regard. I kissed her on the cheek, quick, without grazing her with my sharp teeth. Her eyes closed in reverence.

Several like her had come with me from Nalia after I was cast out. The Far Realm was my last option, and I wouldn't squander it. Maybe working on the mazes was the best use of the day. My mind rebelled, but that wasn't unusual. I was hard to satisfy.

I closed my eyes too.

Circles, angles, measurements, parallel lines, the seductive slip of water from one oval impression in stone to the next...

I sighed and grew reeds to wrap around Lwa's ankles as a

gift. It was magic no one asked for. I liked to wrap them around living limbs. In the caves, among my worshippers, it was a sign of favor.

For those whom my suna lured into the mazes, it meant entrapment.

I released the reeds. Lwa's eyes sparkled with heartfelt thanks.

Laughter bubbled, echoing off the walls. Here on my island centered amid shallow tide pools, I had a good view of the maze entrances, created of stiff reeds as tall as I was. The paths swept in magnificent arcs that changed at my will. Blood and geometry fed me.

It had to be late at night now. Why were they laughing? Had they drunk too much rimbar? Probably. They enjoyed a revel.

Unless...

Women and nymphs, eager to please, had brought me more sacrifices than usual lately. I didn't complain when they attracted leering men guilty of forcing women. Sometimes people simply went missing, after all. But other times, they brought me more innocent males. Rumors said that Lord Hades had begun to notice. I couldn't overstep my welcome here. Although I didn't ask explicitly for anyone (except a few times, again, for guilty blood), my followers wanted to sate me in whatever way possible. I couldn't deny that I ached most of the time for more. They related to that, I suspected, and saw me as a justification for that feeling in them. The males they lured meant revenge or attraction for them just as much as they did for me.

I turned to Lwa's companion, standing a little distance away. She had lighter skin and straight hair the color of a moonless sky. "Did they take another sacrifice?"

She shrugged, uninhibited. "They might have."

I hated the spike of excitement in my belly. "If it is, send him away."

Her answering look was questioning. I rarely sent anyone away if they made it this far through the maze.

I flexed my foot against the rocks to ground myself in my decision. Curiosity and the need clawing inside me were too powerful to stave off for long, though.

"I will see him first."

Lwa and her companion smiled. My satisfaction was theirs. I loved them as they loved me.

Two more females pranced into view on bare feet. They wore simple dresses the green of rock and sea and sky. I knew those movements as their attempt to draw males deeper into the reeds. My reeds—the ones I could wrap around prey with a thought.

He emerged next, an un-self-conscious smile on his face. A male, maybe demi-god since no living humans dwelled in the Far Realm. All manner of creature and deathless, even spirits, but no humans. He was not as tall as I, but he had sharp cheekbones and well-formed shoulders. His skin was the color of old parchment, close to my own. He had no facial hair, but the brown hair on his head had grown long enough to tie up in a knot.

When my followers parted, his mouth went slack. I'd beheld that look many times. Here I was, naked and dangerous, with skin that radiated like flecks in the rock. My short fingernails ended in points (perfect angles) and my hair followed similar lines, long on one side and shorter on the other. Luxurious asymmetry to offset the geometry of the rest of my body—round breasts, oval eyes, twin curves that moved concave to my waist and convex to my hips and thighs.

His gaze didn't move away from me. "Are you a siren?" he breathed.

"I am Aber." I took in my followers with a gesture. "This is my suna."

He appeared to recognize the name and reevaluate the place where he stood. Vaulted natural rock formations rose above us. Tide pools dotted the ground and intricate mazes of reeds grew in a wall behind him. Salty waves crashed with a muffled roar against the cave wall. The tide pools near the exterior cracks filled and spilled into each other.

The male bowed his head.

I readied my reeds, undecided.

"I have heard of your mazes but didn't know they'd be so vast."

My lips stretched into something not quite happy. "Flattery is a poor substitute for sincerity."

My worshippers watched us, enraptured. I'd give them a show while I decided what to do with him.

"I was being sincere." He raised his eyes to mine. They, too, were almond-shaped.

I detected no lie, but I grew a long reed behind him anyway. "I hope so. I respect an honest and upright being. Why did you follow into the reeds?"

He snuffed a self-deprecating laugh. "Your followers are beautiful and offered me a drink. I have no attachments and had no duties today. I thought there might be a party here. I see I should have guessed better." He released a breath. "I'm sorry I intruded."

Honesty again. He didn't deserve to be consumed. "It is no intrusion. They lured you as a sacrifice."

His skin turned pale.

"I will let you go free. Do not fear." I took a measured step forward. Reeds wrapped around his legs.

He looked down in alarm.

"I will let you go free," I repeated. "But first..." I faced him, looking closely at his face, his hair, his body. He smelled like musk and clean soap, not of the ocean. The scent burned along my skin. He didn't quail as he looked back at me. Instead, I saw his pupils widen as he took in again my face and body too.

He wore small golden earrings and had lines between his brows that I found tantalizing.

The reeds snaked up around his legs, which were covered in linen pants. His breathing pattern changed almost as if he were caught between apprehension and desire.

I had no apprehension, but desire grew by the second. His hands had veins on the back. They throbbed at his neck too. I found I didn't want to slice them open, but to enjoy them in other ways.

"You may touch me," I said, leaving his hands free as the reeds slithered higher.

The line between his brows deepened. "What?" For the first time since he'd entered my cave, his gaze darted to the others who watched us. "What do you mean?"

"They like when I am satisfied. You are a beautiful being."

I enjoyed how flustered he became. "So are..."

"If you desire, you may touch me." I drew closer, inhaling his scent. "You may satisfy me here. If you are able."

"Yes," he said quickly.

The plants grew as far as his neck now, tracing a line up the divot of his throat and curving around his beating pulse. His gaze went molten as he leaned into the sensation.

He liked this. Good. So did I.

I willed the reeds around his hips to thicken, to tease between his legs.

His answering expression slickened my core. I could feel the suna getting excited.

He reached out cautiously—another feature I liked about him—and I let my body give him obvious permission.

At first, he slid his strong, veined hands around my sides, dipping down to the curve of my back. He felt warm and eager.

My need roared.

The reeds snapped away. He acted like a person waking from a dream. His hands flew from my skin as if I burned him.

"Touch me," I demanded now. "Come with me."

In a daze, he followed. I had a raised bed of reeds among the tide pools where I took rest. I didn't often have to sleep, but sex was more enjoyable against something softer than stone. It was to this I took him.

"Here," I said. I throbbed. He needed to hurry. I tried not to bare my teeth.

"In front of—?"

"Yes, they watch."

That obviously pleased him. It pleased me too and heightened my pleasure. They knew how to increase my enjoyment and their own.

He drew off his shirt, revealing gleaming muscles beneath. His tied hair came partially undone, loosening flyaways. I sat on the edge of the bed of reeds. Next, he removed his linen pants. Beneath, he was stone-stiff.

I was glad, because I was ready too.

We were strangers, and he didn't know how to touch me. When I opened for him, he took me in like a plan he needed to read before taking action.

"I was told," he said, out of breath already, "that you were bloodthirsty." His hands reached forward and stopped before contacting skin.

I arched to meet his palms, but he drew them just out of reach. "I am."

His gaze flicked beyond me where I knew there were bones. "And that you created all these mazes in the cave."

"I do."

His next words were deliciously husky. "I've never seen anything so impressive. You are every forbidden nightmare."

I could smell my own arousal. I didn't think I wanted him to pause, but this spoken foreplay turned me ravenous.

"Anything I can't do?" He could hardly speak, bending partially over me.

"My reeds will stop you," I said, dry-mouthed, and grabbed his wrist. I gathered him close, my hands climbing around his strong back. My nails grazed his skin, coaxing out the smallest amount of blood.

Finally, he gave into temptation. His palms found my breasts, kneading them as he forced his hips between my legs. My heart pounded, aching for him to enter me. I did it, guiding him in. He gasped, grunting at the sensation.

I wailed as he began thrusting, hard and eager. The rhythm became a chant. He was in. He was deep. Together, we made wet sounds as he rolled his body into mine.

The chant became words spoken by a chorus of high, aroused voices. My followers, watching keenly as I writhed against the reeds.

He hit a sensitive spot that needed friction and—

I yelled out. He strained harder.

A splash left both of us dripping wet. Lwa had thrown a pan of water on us.

The demi-god's long hair, free of its tie, dripped onto my face. Droplets raced down my lips, my belly, my ear, my sides. They felt like fingers and tasted a shade like the blood I'd drawn with my pointed nails.

He bent closer, shoving in, flexing as his hands searched my body. Hot breath blew against my cheek.

Another splash.

I cried out, matching the movement of his hips. We were soaked.

Another splash. Another.

"Fuck!" he gritted out. His rock-hard cock stabbed into me with desperation.

A whimper sounded from the little crowd of a dozen or so.

My mouth opened, sharp teeth showing, but he was in the aching throes of desire. My teeth wouldn't stop him now.

He grunted, rolling his body against mine, touching as much of me as he could with as much of him.

More water poured on us.

We were close, scrabbling and arching and emitting cries of need that echoed through the cave.

Hands. A kiss on my hot cheek. Fingers on my breast.

When the male moaned suddenly, urgently, I opened my eyes. The suna gathered around us, caressing, touching, undulating with our movements.

The sight was almost too much. The sensation catapulted him over the edge. He screamed garbled words as he came hard, first inside me then, after he pulled out, even more over my body. His release was so intense it sounded like pain.

I was so close, needy, angry, throbbing.

He slipped inside me again. I gasped in surprise. Males didn't do that after orgasm. They hadn't before, at least.

Surprise brought me to the brink. Together with my

followers, he touched and flicked, thrusted and kissed until I was a shower of dark light, shaking and arching against the reed bed. Drenched head to foot in sweat, cum, and water, I soaked his cock with my release. I shuddered as I came down from the blistering height.

He pulled out.

My breathing still came out sharp. So did his.

The worshippers didn't stop, instead drawing him in for kisses and caresses. His eyes found me, despite all the intoxicating attention.

I smiled with teeth. Yes, he could revel with us all.

His lids closed as he sank into Lwa's kiss. Clothes dropped into tide pools. The hair falling past his shoulders looked a wet tangle.

As I caught my breath, I noted the symmetrical movements of my followers, the equal attention the sacrifice gave them all. It was like geometry.

He had liked my mazes. And he asked permission before taking. And when he had taken, my body melted into sparks.

I dragged my finger through the cum on my belly and sucked it off.

As I watched him glance back again at me, I hoped he would return to sacrifice himself for our pleasure another day. After this, he would always be welcome at the suna.

6
PREDICTING A KISS

When Ingrid goes to work as a brilliant apothecary's assistant, she notices something different about him.

This original story includes explicit sex, strong language, inexperienced partners, mentor/mentee dynamic, and a romantic crush

The woods of Varafjall turned beautiful in autumn. The heavy heat of the summer that caused many men to work shirtless was swept away by cool breezes. Cinnamon-scented leaves played in the wind. It was a cloudy, mystical time that made work at the apothecary feel sweet. I enjoyed it year-round—Sten said I learned quickly—but the first time reaching for my sweater brought a smile to my face. Apothecaries were meant for autumn. Plus, without the haze of humid summers, time was ripe for augury. Sten had studied that discipline for years. It involved complicated knowledge of trees, water, and birds. I loved watching him get lost in interpretation.

I pushed open the wooden door. Instantly, the air grew warmer. Sten had started a fire in the grate.

He barely glanced up from the assortment of twigs and herbs he was twining together. His eyes—deep-set, serious, and un-self-conscious—had something new in them today. A secret?

I set a lingonberry muffin on the counter beside his work area. "You forget to eat."

"Don't put that on me, Ingrid," he said mildly, not looking up again. "*You* are the one who forgets to eat." With a small smile, there then gone, he reached beneath the counter and set something wrapped in paper next to my muffin.

I peeled back the crinkled paper to reveal a fried ball of dough filled with sheep's cheese. My favorite.

Heat crawled up the sides of my neck. He remembered. I nibbled the dough ball as I took off my scarf.

Sten's busy hands paused their work to snatch the muffin I'd made the night before. I didn't bake often, but the air felt crisp and I wanted to surprise Sten with something.

"I'm bundling herbs," he said between bites. That meant I was supposed to help him.

After washing my hands in a salver in the corner, I joined him at the table. Dried and fresh herbs, all with meanings and combinations that meant healing or curses or divination, laid out before us. The smell intoxicated me. Sten always smelled like this.

He moved easily, sure in his work. From the moment we met four years ago, he'd always been focused on the apothecary, learning as much as he could even though he was already the best in Varafjall. Hrafnir, the god himself, had requested Sten's remedies. I'd been there for that. That day, Sten had gazed levelly back at the king's servant, but as soon as he left, Sten met my eyes and grinned. His grin flipped my insides all around. It was rare, all dimpled lines and disbelief that something good enough had happened to coax it out of him.

He grinned the first time I made the cleansing charm correctly for Winter's Rite. His fingers kept moving over the stems and twigs as if looking for something to adjust. "You've done this perfectly," he declared, and he never declared such a thing unless he meant it.

Sten was not a man for conversation or flattery. A thing was done right or it was re-done. People were too complicated by comparison.

I understood how he felt, though I was more comfortable around others than he was.

As he ate the muffin I made, I bit the inside of my lip to keep from smiling. Once, he said he was only comfortable around me. I wore that sentence like a badge. After that, I started working at the apothecary every day, unless snow or sickness prevented me.

Stuffing the rest of the sheep's cheese ball into my mouth—it tasted salty and savory and all the things I liked—I grabbed twine and set bunches of herbs in front of me on the table, arranged by size and potency. Sten noticed the arrangement. He'd taught it to me.

"To clear the lungs," he explained quietly. Almost too quietly. Sten was never loud, but something obviously preyed on his mind.

I watched him as I worked. His capable shoulders adjusted with each focused movement. We stood close. I could almost feel the heat of him. The silence between us felt full.

"Is everything all right?" My fingers didn't stop gathering and tying bundles in precise configurations.

He pressed his lips together. After a pause, he exhaled through his nose. "Last night, I began the first augury session."

My heartbeat grew heavier. Was something terrible foretold? Usually, Sten divined small things—the shape of weather patterns without exact dates, an image of an event without names or place that only made sense in retrospect...

He didn't elaborate.

I made another bundle. "What did you see?"

His light skin reddened. On his neck, the red turned dark all the way up to his ear and around to his brown hair, which grew to the collar of his shirt. It was often unruly, since work at the apothecary dominated his thoughts, never his appearance. "Nothing clearly."

Sten was quiet, but he'd stopped acting shy around me a long time ago. Our silences were companionable. Now, the space between words scratched like ill-fitting wool clothes.

"You saw something," I challenged. Another bundle of herbs finished, I set it with his completed ones.

"Sometimes the signs are meant to confuse. It's the job of the augur to interpret, and I can't interpret yet."

"You can tell me." I looked up at him encouragingly. The more he avoided explaining his unease, the more I burned to know. "Maybe I can help you."

His lips twitched in a rueful smile. He didn't look at me. "You're the only person I would tell if I could. But the spirits are preying on my weaknesses."

I frowned at him. Blood surged through my veins. Something wasn't right. "What weaknesses?" No one I knew was half as talented as Sten. His shyness wasn't a weakness, only a feature.

With a sigh, he paused his work at last to look at me. Just a look, brief, before he looked down.

My skin and core went hot. So much threaded through that look. Did I just want it to mean more?

He stood gazing thoughtfully at the ground for too long. It gave me time to notice the natural curve of his lips, the strength of his neck and shoulders, the grace of his hands with their long, skilled fingers. Sten was all warmth and natural beauty that would be inviting if he weren't so single-minded in his work. It was a privilege to work beside him and learn. I'd accepted long ago that he wouldn't see me as more.

"I saw..." He swallowed uncomfortably. "I saw a picture of me. With someone." Finally, he raised his eyes. "With you."

A bolt speared my heart. I tried not to react. "We're always together," I said, giving him a way out of admitting anything embarrassing. My words came out breathy.

He tapped his hand against his thigh unconsciously. "This was different."

"The first time you've seen yourself."

"No." The seriousness in his expression caught me off guard.

"Were you... bothered?" I guessed. *Please don't be disgusted by the idea of us together.*

He thought for a heartbeat before shaking his head.

The headiness of his scent made it difficult to continue acting uninterested. If I admitted the depth of my feelings for him, he might never feel comfortable working with me again. I couldn't risk it.

"I tried to interpret all night. It was always the same. I don't know what to make of it." He looked pained. "I wasn't going to tell you. There's no need for... awkwardness." His throat worked as he pivoted back to the counter.

Disappointment swelled in my gut. Sten had all but called me his weakness, but he hadn't said why. The intensity behind his gaze spoke the truth. What was I supposed to do with that knowledge? The idea that somewhere in his soul Sten wanted me, that the spirits could plague him with an image of us together, would snare my mind through autumn and winter and spring and summer nights. The gentle folds of his soft sleeves would haunt me more than they already, passively, did.

Reluctantly, I reached for more herbs for the lung remedy. In the silence, only the crackle of the small fire, the rasp of ingredients drawn across the wooden tabletop, and the hushed sounds of breathing filled the room.

Though I tried not to look at Sten, I sensed him paying attention to my presence, just like I paid attention to his.

I had to re-bind a bundle of herbs. When it was ready, I placed it atop the work he had already done.

He finished at the same time. Our hands formed an avoidant conversation. I placed my bunch down first, then he did.

Instead of efficiently returning to the task, I left my hand hovering close.

The choice felt monumental, an offer. I'd leave it there a few seconds, not long. I could still pull back. Nothing needed to happen. Neither of us needed to admit anything.

Sten was nothing if not single-minded in his work. But he didn't continue either.

I felt weightless.

With the care of an animal approaching danger, Sten's large hand moved over the pile of herbs toward mine. He paused a breath away from touching.

Blushing furiously, my insides a wreck of knots, I tapped the side of my hand against his.

Emboldened, he folded his hand over mine. It was

awkward and endearing, not quite holding hands, but declaring his intention to do so.

Breathing used to be easier. The room used to be cooler.

Sten wanted to hold my hand. He was disturbed when the spirits identified his weakness, and his weakness... was me.

I stood, trying to catch my breath. Then, rallying my courage, I looked up at him.

Such earnest care and uncertainty lived in his face that I thought I might dissolve. A puddle on the floor of the apothecary, never to revive again.

I rotated my hand so it fit against his, palm to palm. We threaded our fingers together. Sweat coated my palm. Did he mind? I wanted to feel his capable hands flush against my skin for as long as he'd allow.

We still faced the work counter. But now he leaned toward me. His arm molded against mine. Delicious heat spread down my body as he pressed closer.

This was a dream. This wasn't real. Sten wasn't tipping his face close enough to mine that I had to close my eyes.

Soft lips met mine. A sweet press, and then it was over.

My eyes went huge. He still had a question in his, but lightness, happiness, ghosted his features.

I wanted more. Now that I knew I could have more with Sten, all the feelings I'd practiced pushing down swelled up. My skin felt hot and needy. His torso, strong but not bulky, was suddenly important. His soft, masculine features coaxed me closer with a force that almost made me afraid.

We peeled away from the counter to face each other more fully. This was more important. Our hands never unlinked.

"Was it this?" I breathed. "That you saw?"

Face alight, he shook his head no.

I felt dizzy. The place between my legs throbbed, slick and sensitive. Tentatively, I moved forward.

With his usual seriousness, Sten met me before I reached him. Our next kiss lingered, warm and wanting. He slipped a hand around my back, holding me against him. The firm column of his body felt like the hearth after a cold day. I yearned for him so much that I missed his lips before they'd left mine. I wanted those skilled hands, that sweet intensity, all of him for as long as I could have him. I wanted him so much I ached.

Sten was almost too careful, but I wouldn't rush him. He didn't run into these kinds of encounters—if he'd ever had one before. It was difficult to picture. He was so precise and intense about everything he did, obsessive even, that relationships weren't casual to him. He didn't need them. He had the work.

Kissing me meant the work could wait, and the work was his life.

I moved more insistently against his mouth, parting my lips in case he wanted to experiment with more passion. He answered, licking inside. A moan escaped my throat. At the noise, he stiffened under my hands. Had I gone too far? I felt his heart beat thick and fast through his shirt.

An inhaled breath and then he turned me so my lower back hit the counter. His heavy body followed, pinning me there.

It was perfect. It was everything. I wanted to feel him and he let me feel it all.

My fingers slipped into his hair as he bent me backward, still sucking kisses from my lips. My pulse ran like a rabbit's. Desperation to keep going made me hold him closer, harder.

Our kisses were wet and messy now. Sten desired me. The

same intensity I saw in him every day now focused entirely on me.

When he rolled his hips, a hard bulge stroked between my legs. I gasped.

Something shifted in him. Hands clutched, teeth grazed my lip, and he ground himself against me again. At my waistline, he stilled. A question.

I nodded against him.

He dove down. I panted, struggling to comprehend what was happening.

"Show me where," he said.

"It's... it's easier when..." I pulled my pants down so I could guide his hand. He held out two fingers stiff as an arrow. With them, I dug through the labia. His concentration nearly broke me. All the single-mindedness he reserved for learning remedies now pivoted to learning me.

When his fingers skimmed my clit, I jolted.

"There? Here? This?" He rubbed it again, not needing me holding his closed hand anymore.

A whimper was my only answer.

He continued in perfect circles. I squirmed against the table. "Oh! This...!"

"What about this?" He changed the rhythm. Instead of circles, he made quick, up and down rubbing movements.

I spasmed, knees nearly buckling. He caught me. Bolts of pleasure arced out from his fingers to my extremities. I begged incoherently against his chest. He didn't stop. He didn't even slow.

I dripped onto his hand and I would come if he didn't stop. It was too messy, too embarrassing...

"Stop," I squeaked.

Heaving like a runner, he slowed and pulled his fingers away. They glistened.

"Stop?"

"Go," I said, kissing him. The trousers around my knees made my steps tiny.

Relief made his kisses smoother. He tasted like lingonberry.

"Not over here," he said, smothered by my mouth on his.

The working station. We couldn't destroy the clean table.

We stumbled together toward a bench against the wall. On long days, we sat there, usually in silence after our legs finally got tired. It wasn't particularly comfortable, but it would do.

"Can I...?" His hand fitted around my bare hip and slid between my legs again. He paused at my inner thigh, waiting for me.

"Yes." Maybe here I wouldn't mind coming all over him.

We slumped gracelessly onto the bench as he found my clit again as if it was nothing. I shook, mouth open, unable to ground myself. Sten held me with his other arm like I was a project that he'd finish, no matter what happened.

My whimpers turned to cries. He kept the pressure, never lost the exact angle I needed.

Embarrassment be damned. I squirted, soaking his hand, as a blinding orgasm took me down.

My cheeks burned when I met his eyes again, but they were glazed, his whole scholar's body radiating lust. My center pulsed again, eager for him.

"Sten..."

He crawled on top of me, loosening the front of his pants. I watched, fascinated, as he pulled them down. Our position wasn't great. His movements weren't practiced, but he attempted to be efficient as he did with everything. I didn't care. This was perfection to me.

His cock, hard and veiny, jutted out. He gripped it, briefly checking in with me. Again, I nodded.

He began near my clit, which was slippery with cum.

"Lower," I managed.

He dragged the head of his cock down my seam. I was desperate, flexing around nothing, needing him to fill me.

When he sank into my warm pussy, his mouth opened in indecent pleasure.

"Yes," I said, trying to adjust my hips so give him a better angle.

He pushed in further. Excitement took over and he thrust, slow at first, then faster.

I wanted to laugh or burst or fly.

His brow furrowed as he plowed into me, his face and neck bright red. Sweat began at his temple.

We worked together, learning, filling the gaps, doing all the things we did with innocent work now transformed into something breathless and craving. I never wanted anyone more. Now apparently allowed, I ran my hands over his body. He still wore clothes on the top half and so did I, but that didn't mean I couldn't reach beneath his shirt and feel the muscles there. A fuzz of hair covered them. My fingers and palm bumped over his nipple. He felt warm and real and so fucking sensual that I barely kept my head.

He made a pained noise and pulled out, splashing cum over my front. Some hit my belly, bared by the rhythmic motions against the bench, but most was still covered by a shirt.

I laughed.

Sitting up on his knees, Sten held his dick loosely in one hand. He looked unbearably sexy, flushed and proud.

He grinned. Such unapologetic joy shone in his face that my throat grew claggy.

His smile faltered. "What's wrong?" His gaze dipped. "I destroyed your shirt."

"It doesn't matter." I hooked him for another kiss.

"It does. I'll get you another one."

I sat up. We fixed our clothes, staying close enough to feel each other's breath. His lingonberry no doubt smelled better than my sheep's cheese, but he leaned in anyway.

When we were finally able to stand, clothing in place, he kissed my hot cheek. If this had happened a couple weeks ago, I would have melted from the heat. Autumn was truly a godblessed time.

"Is that what you saw?" I asked.

He blushed all over again. His serious expression had the softness of relief about it, though. "Only an image."

His talented finger ran down my side to my hip.

"I see." Mouth dry, I stood breathing beside him for a while longer.

Sten sighed. "I don't know... what this means." His gaze flicked to the table with the herbs on it. He liked his days focused. I'd thrown that off.

We'd both obviously enjoyed that, but did this mean we'd become too much of a distraction for each other? I couldn't lose the apothecary. I couldn't lose Sten. Especially now. "What do you want it to mean?"

He searched my face. My belly squirmed. "That... It was..." His eyes glazed as he tried to find words.

I took his hand and nodded. "It was."

His cheek crinkled. "If you let me, I'll do it again, better."

My center pooled. Feeling bold, I cupped his jaw. "I'll let you tomorrow and all the days after that."

His lashes fluttered. "I need to concentrate." He meant on work. If he hadn't said it so helplessly, I might have pitied him. But all I felt was delight.

"We can," I said with conviction I didn't feel. "We have work to do."

Seeing him look to me for guidance, first about my body and now about anything related to his apothecary work, left me buoyant. He was the great Sten. He didn't care what people thought or did. All he cared about was his own efficiency and curiosity. And now, me.

He seemed to gain resolve. "To clear the lungs," he said, almost to himself.

"Yes." I steered him toward the salver to wash. He went first, rubbing my cum from his fingers. He stared at his hands as he moved through his mechanical method of washing. I copied him and then we returned to the bench where he'd fingered me. I couldn't look at the slightly mussed pile of dried herbs the same way. "We can do this," I said.

He noticed the way the herbs were slightly askew too. "Can we do it tonight? If you're not busy."

I chuckled. I meant the task in front of us. We could take one reasonable step forward, but his mind was filled with me.

If you're not busy... I was never busy. The apothecary—and Sten—dominated all my time. After work, I went home, ate a quick supper, and slept.

"Tonight is perfect. Do you want to come over? I have a bed," I teased. "And food." Asking him felt surreal. He was untouchable, wonderful from afar.

"I have a bed and food too." Then he appeared to catch my tone. "But, I would love to come over."

We faced the table with our unfinished work on it. Unable to help myself, I reached for his hand, finding his on its way to me. We tangled fingers and bumped our shoulders against each other.

This time, the silence felt warm and kind, charged and focused.

We both forgot to eat.

7
MOUNTING THE SIREN

Elu the siren has returned, and Valen is there to meet him.

This original story includes explicit monster sex, strong language, and the mention of violence

I practiced rolling the word around in my mouth. *Hello.* But it didn't sound like hello. It sounded like warmth and water and song.

I had Abaddon's own time trying to find any reference to the language of sirens. Male sirens, specifically. They had their own means of communication since they were sea-bound and their more violent female counterparts lived mostly on shore.

After last year's encounter with Elu, the magnificent siren fighting his own biology to escape his brother's grisly fate, I had more than enough excuse to lose myself in my obsession. Merpeople, sirens, their habits and lives, biology and language. When I wasn't patrolling dangerous corners of the Far Realm to keep the peaceful beings safe, I was at home. Nearly once a month, I traveled to Nyx. They'd built a new library open at all hours so that nocturnal species could study too. The Library of Nyx, seven stories and filled with everything from dangerous, semi-sentient scrolls to silly stories for children, turned out to be the best resource I'd ever found to discover more about sirens. My friends wondered why I didn't drink with them anymore.

Instead, I drank in information about the siren who said he'd meet me again in this spot, during this mating season.

Had we agreed we'd have sex again? He'd implied it, at least.

Danger on the job couldn't freeze my breath like the memory of that moment. All my filthiest forbidden fantasies came true that day. And they could come true again.

I tried saying the siren word for *hello* out loud again. It sounded sloppy coming out of my mouth. Was I acting too desperate?

A ridiculous laugh burst out at that. Of course I was. But I'd been desperate last year too, yet Elu had welcomed me with an outstretched hand and one word: "Come."

Oh, and I had. Hard.

I wasn't on patrol today. Glancing out from the overhang of the house toward the savage stretch of beach, I saw no one. Good. We couldn't be interrupted. Mating with sirens wasn't explicitly forbidden by law, but it was social taboo. If we were caught, they'd think he forced me. If anything, I came onto him. And then he agreed. And then we fucked like I'd never dared to dream would happen outside my imagination.

My survey of the water didn't show Elu either. He was coming, wasn't he?

I straightened my cuffs and loose pants. No gear today. I wanted everything soft and easy to take off. I was no beauty, one of those demi-goddesses that came out different than everyone else. Some of us were tiny or webbed or scaly or animal in appearance. With the deathless, you never knew. The most common deathless look was... Well, it was like Elu—tall and gorgeous, muscled like a statue.

My chest felt tight. He had to be on his way here. I walked back under the house, which had been built on pylons. The cold, wet sand of the beach gave way to rock where the abandoned structure molded to a stone outcropping. Underneath was a cave. I visited the cave often. Yes, it was cold and trapped me at highest tide, but the floor was smooth and the memories intoxicating as wine.

My lips pursed as I turned back to the wild Stygian Sea waves sliding up almost to the rock. Siren mating season was called a season because it wasn't only one day. It took a while. Those in charge of safety, like me, had to work extra to make sure no one wandered close. Female sirens acted more bloodthirsty than usual during that time.

Because of that, Elu had agreed to mate with me instead, so he could return to the sea unharmed.

Secretly, I hoped he saw it as more than that.

I did.

A tail thrashed above the waterline.

My heart jumped into my throat. I knew that tail. It was the one I saw in dreams. I ran to the mouth of the cave to watch Elu as he emerged.

He arched up, dripping and so fucking glorious that I forgot how to breathe. Water streamed from his green locks, which fell past his shoulder. In the dimness of the storm last time, I hadn't seen his skin well. It was green too, the gray-green of deep water. My heart rammed against my ribcage.

With a mighty wave of his tail, which threw up foam and water, he propelled himself onto the shore. He didn't see me.

Patience was shit. I didn't want to wait. I wanted to run toward him, and, if he were a different being, I would have wrapped my arms around his broad shoulders.

I wasn't typically one for romance. It didn't interest me. At least, it hadn't. If all Elu and I did was fuck once a year, that was enough for me. But I could be greedy too. If he'd give me more, I'd take it.

Elu caught himself on his wide hands, pushing himself up. Gods, that view of his chest...

We finally locked eyes.

"You came back." I clasped my hands together to keep from grabbing his arm to help him up. That was a stupid impulse. Sirens didn't get up. But it did look like it cost him a lot of effort to walk forward on his hands with his enormous tail flapping behind.

"We agreed," he said in that voice I remembered.

Which reminded me.

"*Hello*," I said in what I hoped now was his language. The books could have been wrong. My attempt to mimic the pronunciation could have been wrong. The word could have been a ridiculous combination of noises and not a word at all.

He paused and regarded me. His look was alien, no recognizable emotion in his face at first. But then, with a slap of his tail, a smile. "*Hello*."

I sucked in a deep breath. In most situations, I felt grounded, competent. Here, I felt like I tottered on the edge of a cliff, ready to fall any second.

I'd gotten the word right. I made a fist of victory, but tried to keep it subtle.

He struggled forward, muscles straining. As beautiful as the sight was, he didn't need to keep dragging himself into the cave. He'd reached the cave—half in, half out, really—which made him easier to spot from the beach, but I didn't care about that anymore. My entire body zinged with anticipation.

"You don't need to come all the way to where you were last time," I said before realizing the sentence was a more complex one. Elu spoke some of my language, but had no reason to learn much. "You can stop," I revised.

He did, angling on one elbow. That position looked more comfortable for him. It was painful, how beautiful he was. I knew, just like I knew last year, that my obsessive attention made me a creep. I swallowed, taking in the shape of his chest and the seamless way his skin melded into the sleek scales of his tail. The light was better than last year, and the sight of him nearly made me emotional.

"I'm glad you're here," I said thickly.

Elu canted his head, face unreadable again. "Valen."

My pulse pounded wet between my legs.

"I am glad too." Then—*gods and the Divine!*—he eased himself down onto his back and drew up his tail. He reached backward for me.

I toyed with the idea of keeping my clothes on and making Elu take them off, but in case he couldn't pause the mating cycle long enough to do that, I decided not to risk it. I stripped everything off.

As soon as I got close enough to grab, he fished me in with wet, strong hands and pinned me to his seat. It felt like a throne to me, his tail arched high, flexing against the entire column of naked back. He pulled my legs apart so I straddled him. Was he surprised that I had taken off *everything*? Female sirens were monsters, but they were beautiful monsters. I was only me.

If he was surprised, he didn't show it. This time, I wanted to feel even more of him against my skin. His fingers splayed against my thighs, hard, so I couldn't move. When sirens mated, it was desperate, a biological need so strong they risked death.

I was glad he didn't want to waste time either.

I sucked in a salt-scented breath as something tickled my entrance. His first long cock emerged from the hidden slit in his skin to swim up into me. This sensation! I refused to feel self-conscious as I grabbed Elu's tail where it rose above my head and closed my eyes just to feel him. On its own, the member slithered deeper.

I'd learned another word: *yes*. The musicality of it didn't come through very well as I said it in a strangled moan.

Elu's hands tightened on my thighs. When I opened my eyes to see his expression, he echoed the word back. Some of the same feral need I remembered from last time shone in his carved face, but his eyes were less fearful and more desiring. This wasn't a race to orgasm before his partner ate him. This was being so turned on we both barely knew where we were. The knowledge that he felt safer than before made my insides flutter around his now growing cock.

This was the only uncomfortable part, and even this I craved, I dreamed about. He thickened and hardened, his cock transforming from snake to stone. At least that was what it felt like. He wedged me open, stretching my walls. Every part of me was him. If I hadn't been so godsdamned sopping, it would have been excruciating.

I whimpered.

His dick rammed inside me. Sirens didn't need to thrust. Their cocks did that for them. As long as I didn't move, he could punch up into me.

My body convulsed. His didn't loosen his grip. He hurt, he took, he—

A small, hard second cock vibrated against my clit. Perfectly positioned. Perfectly stimulating.

Hades and all the gods!

Sounds I didn't recognize burst from my mouth as I twisted against the friction. My nipples were hard beads. My fingers dug into the solid muscle of Elu's tail. He was relentless, pounding into me and bringing me to the edge of blackout orgasm.

I peeled my eyes open. I couldn't miss his face. The intensity I'd seen before was nothing. He practically glowed as he watched.

For him to come, I had to first. Biology. I wouldn't make him wait. I *couldn't* wait.

Straining and shuddering, I came all over him. Pleasure darted to my fingertips, my legs, and up to the points of my breasts. Everything burst open with aching release.

Elu's breathing grew fiercer, a swimmer in a race. With a guttural sound that rumbled through my frame, he came too. The massive cock stuck inside me shot heavy, warm streams.

I sighed, contentment filling me like syrup.

He shoved me off him. I was empty, but I wasn't surprised. He'd done the same last time—compulsion since siren mates would often cannibalize their partners after sex.

"Elu," I said quickly. It would take no time at all for him to roll back into the water and disappear for another year. Mere minutes was too short.

He looked at me, intense but bleary with the sex we'd just had. His cocks were retracting into his skin. I wanted to watch them, to know everything about his body and his life when he wasn't compelled to shore, but I only had today.

"Do you know what a kiss is?"

Stupid question, probably. To him, mouths meant teeth, and teeth meant danger.

But he didn't leave. "No." His curiosity didn't look like other people's. He didn't quirk a brow. He just waited, very still, without judgment.

"It's a loving gesture on shore," I said. "We touch our lips together—there's no biting." Some people kissed more vigorously than others, but I didn't say that. I, for one, would not bite him.

He looked skeptical.

The rock was hard under my knee where he'd pushed me to the ground. "I like when we... do that. A kiss means we enjoy each other."

His smaller cock disappeared under his skin.

"If I get close to you now, would you pin me to your seat again?" His tail wasn't angled up, the signal that he was ready to mate. Instead, it lingered thick and long behind him, the fin waving lazily.

"No, I would not."

"I like you, Elu," I ventured. The cold from the cave replaced the heat of being with the siren, and bumps crawled over my skin.

"I like you, Valen."

Okay. I never thought I'd heard those words. Not from anyone and *definitely* not from a being like Elu. He was everything I never dared to hope for.

He couldn't know how much weight I felt in those words. They were more dangerous than siren teeth.

"Honestly?" I asked, rising to my feet.

"I thank you," he said. "I like you." He dashed green hair back over his shoulder.

"May I kiss you? I'll be careful."

A smile teased one side of his mouth. *Oh gods, could he get any more stunning?* "Be careful with your lips."

I laughed, on the verge of hysteria. "I will."

Slowly, I approached, watching Elu's hand. During mating, he would grab me, but he didn't do that now.

I lowered beside him. Because he was so large, I didn't need to go down far to meet his eye line. Such beautiful eyes. They watched me as I reached gently for his cheek. It was smooth, wet, and warm. I traced his cheekbone with my thumb.

My heartbeat sped. Trying to savor the moment, not to rush, I studied him. Had anyone gotten this close to a living male siren? I doubted anyone had gazed into their eyes like this. Elu was brave. He kept promises. He was sexy as sin.

My gaze dropped to his lips, which were unfairly full and masculine. Keeping my own lips tightly together so my teeth didn't show, I leaned in. His lips met mine. I exhaled, pressing just a little harder.

Elu smelled like the sea—not that rotting scent so often on shore, but the *sea,* like freedom and space and heaving waves and endless skies. Like salt and breeze and dangerous waters.

I stayed there, my lips against his, taking him in, dizzy from the rush of it.

Elu hummed. It sounded like a contented noise, but I couldn't be sure. He scooped me closer with one strong arm. I smiled, closed-mouthed, against him. Now his muscled chest lay flush against my bare one.

I could stay here forever.

His mouth didn't move much during the kiss, but enough to know he was paying attention to the shape of mine. I didn't want to scare him by sucking and nipping and all the things I would have loved to do in that moment. This was more than enough.

I took advantage of our closeness and pressed my chest against him, traced his shoulder with my palm, cupped the muscles of his back. I found a small raised scar there. I felt like the best kind of explorer.

Again, he heaved me closer, this time on top of him, but it wasn't the same as the mating ritual. He didn't pin me to his lap; he draped me over him. His firm body breathed and flexed under me. Our lips never separated.

This was almost too good to enjoy in the moment. I kept doubting it was really happening.

His fingers tensed on my back. He pulled out of the kiss, far enough that I could see the hint of wildness in his eyes. "Off, or again," he said hoarsely.

Behind me, his tail had drawn up.

I smiled, holding back a toothy grin. "Again."

IF YOU LIKED THIS STORY, FIND MORE ABOUT VALEN AND Elu in *Lovers and Monsters*!

8
FINISHING THE ENEMY

An obsession with defeating a long-time enemy turns into more after a life-threatening injury.

This original story includes explicit M/M sex, strong language, verbally abusive parents, blood, hate sex, dub-con, mention of war, enemies to lovers, and violence

I pulled my arms through the sleeves of my father's dark blue formal jacket. Fabric stretched tight over my biceps. As the measurements had already shown, my arms were larger than his had been, but my chest wasn't as broad.

The tailor made a note on a pad of paper before bowing slightly from the waist. He was human, not deathless, but I'd been ruling a short enough time to use only this tailor for every adjustment. He knew fabric and metal, clothes and armor.

Glancing in the polished bronze mirror, I curled my lip at the ill-fitting suit. I looked like my father—beard, intense eyes, lightly tanned skin. Just last week, I'd gone to my father's suna to visit his worshippers. Looking at his statue grounded me and reminded me again that I had inherited and earned the small walled province of Eptah. I was Lord Rex's son. No one at the suna knew that my father never respected me. They only knew I was Teo, the new ruler, worthy of similar, though less fervent, adoration. They looked to me to protect them from the raids and sieges. And I would, despite my formidable enemy.

While alive, Father reminded me regularly that I should be more like General Lybus' son, the better fighter, the more charming, the braver, more intelligent...

"Can you add leather shoulder guards to this?" I asked, turning away. I indicated with my hand. "With a higher neck?"

The tailor bent his head. "Of course. As you wish."

I discussed details a little longer, trying to conjure the image of Andros to describe exactly what I wanted. Andros had outfitted the people bringing provisions to his army outside the walls with this feature, making it much harder to kill them. When I looked for Andros next, he wore one too.

Would he mock my decision to copy his choice?

I paused. It didn't matter. A good leader searched for ways to improve regardless of the source.

I left my father's jacket with the tailor and headed for the training yard. Andros had breached the city wall a month ago. He was due to try again. All reports confirmed movement.

He could be defeated, I reminded myself. His maddening way of treating my legacy as a game, as if Eptah belonged to him, stoked the fire in my blood. He was a son of the city, but he had no right to rule it. Every loss, every time we were pushed back or a plan went wrong because my opponent was a fucking genius in strategy, my father's voice returned to me.

Despite his frustrations with me, I knew I could defeat Andros. We were demi-gods. He could be killed.

When we were growing up, hand to hand sparring was usually done outside. Northern Zenia had a temperate climate most of the year, so it made sense. More people could train at a time. Since the attacks had worsened, though, I moved all training inside. The sight of the empty space, overgrown with grass and weeds, twisted something inside me.

Passing through the rounded door, I focused instead at the task at hand—keeping my body sharp and reflexes fast. It smelled like sweat and wax inside. Only a handful of others practiced during these off hours. The sound of their scuffles and hard breathing echoed off the walls.

Soldiers parted for me as I strode the length of the polished floor and entered a side room to change. This—stripping down to the waist and pulling on soft, flexible trousers to fight—felt more natural than the dignified outfits and speeches belonging to my father. I wanted Eptah, but keeping it felt like holding water in a closed fist. I'd rescue one part, but more kept leaking away. Anger, determination, and, most of all, sheer spite, kept me on my feet. I heaved in a slow breath and faced the door to the main sparring room. No weapons today. Only hand to hand.

Emerging from the room, I accepted a long strip of cloth from an attendant to wrap my hands. I needed to feel the give of flesh, the sting of pain. Maybe that would jolt me into ideas for better defense.

A bitter chuckle formed in my throat. The only advisor truly qualified to help was Andros himself. He knew this place like I did, all its hiding places and vulnerabilities. I sought advice from my father's consultants, but they didn't know what to do against someone like this. Most of the time, all we could do was react and pray that was enough.

I clapped my hands together and lowered into a series of stretches. As soon as I closed my eyelids, Andros appeared behind them, younger, in this very building. It was part memory and part nightmare formed from what came after.

"That's all you can do?" He smirked and bent into a deeper stretch over his leg. His torso touched his thigh as he gripped his bare foot, first on one side, then the other.

When he raised his head, all ferocity and freckles and keen intelligence, I knew he was ready to fight.

I stood. We'd done this many times.

"Let's go."

Before the words completely left my mouth, he was on me with a jab. I only half-defended myself before centering, feigning, and jabbing at his jaw.

The blended memory became all the times we had fought and honed each other's skills until we dripped sweat and blood. Neither of us wanted to admit defeat. Early on, as children, one of us would win, the other concede. I conceded more often until my father got wind of our practices and mocked my failure. After that dressing down, I refused to yield to the general's son. I still bore scars and injuries from that time. Pain tolerance too. Because much of it was pain. Andros was better and he knew it. He'd make bets about how many times he could hit me, how fast I'd go down. He'd grin when I got angry.

Fuck that smile.

I released the last in the series of stretches and jumped to my feet. One of the trainers was set to spar with me this afternoon. I didn't see him.

The cloth felt tight around my closed fist. It was like nothing fit, just this endless fight for survival and reign.

Spotting the trainer, I stalked toward him, ready to hit something.

"Scouts are on the move."

"It will be any day."

"We can't store more than three months' worth of food. If a siege lasts longer than that..."

The trainer and I barely spoke. I threw myself into practice, rotating through techniques. I earned a few victories. This man was no Andros. Remembering Andros' moves, I adjusted the angle of my next hit and made satisfying contact. Damn it, even here, in one of the places I felt most like myself, Andros dictated every movement, every thought.

I roared, advancing, trying to banish the image of that hateful grin.

When would I do enough to make my father proud? Well, he couldn't be proud anymore. I'd lost that chance. All I had to do now was defeat Andros. That would at least be enough to make myself proud.

An urgent noise outside, in the direction of the empty courtyard, caught my attention. No windows looked out on it, but all the sparring partners paused.

"What was that?" I demanded.

Before anyone could obey and look outside, four blood-streaked warriors entered. I couldn't tell where the blood was coming from. They all moved as if unhurt.

"What?" I said, more loudly. My heart ran heavy and fast in my chest. "What happened?"

But I knew what happened. Andros' forces had returned. I didn't even have any weapons strapped to me, just adrenaline and the duty to act right away.

"Andros," one said, snapping to attention before me. Her leather and metal armor didn't have the high neck I'd requested of the tailor. A liability. Everything I did felt like plugging up the holes in my fingers before all the water ran out. Nothing was good enough.

"What about him?" I asked, too harshly.

Her dirty face lifted in a savage look of triumph. "He's dead, my lord."

My breath stopped. It couldn't be. I scanned the rest of their faces to discover if this was a cruel joke. They wore the same expressions.

"He was mine!" I shouted. I was supposed to finish him. No one else.

The woman flinched at my outburst. A man beside her spoke up. "He's dying. We captured him. He's bleeding out. We came to tell you, my lord."

My air came in gusts at this news. "Where?"

"The dungeon. Solitary."

Andros was under my fortress, locked in the room with no light or access to the outside world. Could he escape from there? Would his followers somehow plan to free him?

The soldier said he was bleeding out. How much time did he have? What if I didn't make it in time?

"If you want to see him, my lord," said the woman, "I suggest you go quickly."

I was moving before making the decision to go. Flinging the door open, I squinted at the afternoon light. I was a chaos. The elation I anticipated didn't come. Urgency and questions were all I had.

The warriors followed me out. For the first time in a long time, I cursed the magical wards that protected the city. They prevented any deathless being from traveling through the air in or out. I couldn't simply appear by the fortress. I had to walk.

I held my hand out. "Knife."

Someone obliged.

The fortress sat on the hill, up from the tailor's and the training area. The city lay behind me. I marched forward, eating up the distance between me and my enemy.

"Where's the army?" I asked. We were in the open but I was past caring who heard about these matters.

"In retreat."

"Make sure."

"Yes, my lord."

From the corner of my eye, I saw one of the soldiers peel off to follow orders.

I hurried toward the outside access to the dungeon, flanked by two guards. They unlocked the door when they saw me coming. I tripped lightly down the stairs, descending into darkness.

I reserved this place for the very worst, the ones deserving of torture, and there weren't enough here at the moment to create much noise. Even the smell was more dank than rancid. Clutching the knife in my fist, I turned toward the lone cell at the end of the hall. A metal door blocked its occupant completely from view.

Andros.

Andros.

Andros.

His name was a drumbeat in my ears. What if he had already bled out? What if he was gone?

"Unlock the door."

A male warrior stepped forward with a key. He turned it in

the lock and scraped the heavy door back over the stone floor with a horrible shriek. Blackness lay within.

"I need a light," I said, hating my own breathlessness.

The shuffling feet of the soldiers stopped me from hearing any noise from inside the cell. No mocking words or gasps of pain emerged. My ribcage seemed to tighten around my lungs.

Someone handed me a metal lantern. The rays of light showed a hay-strewn stone floor within, and the outline of a few large stones on the wall, criss-crossed with etched words or drawings. To see the entire space, I'd have to open the door all the way or step inside. "Stay here."

Three years felt like no time and an eternity, but it was enough to make these soldiers understand that I needed this moment with my opponent alone. I had a lantern and a knife. And, as they said, Andros was bleeding to death, maybe already dead, so he posed less of a threat. Until he drew his final breath, I'd never say he posed no threat.

They closed the door behind me.

I held the lantern high to cast more light. The faint scent of hay and piss floated on the air, and on top of that, a newer odor. Metallic, and something else I couldn't name but knew as well as my home.

Andros sat slumped against the far wall, his limbs messy and head drenched in blood. His hands, folded in his lap, looked stained and worn with use. He filled out leather armor scored by blades. One cut sliced the neck guard. I tensed. He wasn't above acting injured to catch me by surprise.

He met my eyes with a twinkle of amusement.

Alive, then.

Slightly dizzy, I palmed the knife. Nights of fantasizing what I wanted to do to him, and now he was all mine. Bloody. Alone.

"Still scared of me?" His eyes fell to my wrapped hand, now holding the blade. A smirk played on the edges of his lips.

Did nothing rattle him? Rage reared up, heating my neck. "I never was."

"Bullshit." His voice, mid-tone, usually so clear, sounded sunken. He held my gaze.

I didn't contradict him. Here, I was in the power position. Instead, I set down the lantern, throwing crazy shadows on the cell walls. It felt better to have a hand free. With the light coming from another direction, Andros' injury became clearer. A head wound, but it didn't look like he'd suffered anything else.

All those nights, and now I didn't know what to do. Ending him quickly would have been anti-climactic. But if I didn't, he'd die anyway at the rate he was bleeding. I didn't want hesitation, but it stuffed my senses anyway, suffocating me.

"Don't tell me you're reminiscing," said Andros. "It's a bad time."

"Shut up."

He did look too pale. White and dark red with patches of brown freckles on his face. They always got darker in the summer. When we were younger, I thought they looked reckless. Now that we were grown demi-gods who hadn't been this close in years, they looked rugged. Earned, almost.

I set my jaw hard. "Here, there are two options. I kill you now for what you've done, or I save your life."

His eyebrows rose. "You want to keep me, do you?"

His apparent surprise struck me. It was stupid to assume he'd understand exactly what I was thinking, but after all this time, he felt omniscient to me. He could guess my thoughts when we were young, friends, rivals, distant acquaintances, and finally blood enemies. Maybe he didn't know everything after all.

There was something inevitable about my saving him. What was I without him to vanquish? He could rot in this cell and I could feel the rush of victory over and over again. Strange that I hadn't felt it yet.

"You have answers that I need," I said, clipped. Irritation made my movements jagged, but I laid the knife against my palm to slice the wrapping off.

A slow, feline smile spread across Andros' face. His eyelids drooped and eyes unfocused, betraying the fact that all his bravado covered up that he was a quickly dying man.

I dropped to my knees beside him. "Don't think about moving," I hissed.

He raised a finger languidly in acknowledgement.

"Is it just the head?" I moved sticky hair off of his forehead to examine the wound. He needed water and some other things, but my mercy only extended so far.

His mouth twitched down in a private joke. I clamped my teeth together, annoyance growing. "Yes," he answered. "Your people couldn't manage to touch anything else."

I paused daubing the wound, nasty-looking but shallow. Not as bad as I'd thought. "By the fucking God-King!" I roared. "Why can't you leave me alone? Stop terrorizing us."

"Can't take any competition?" This time, real menace laced his words. The reason for his aggression lay just underneath.

"This isn't a game," I growled, already regretting my decision as I wound the light-colored cloth around his head to stanch the bleeding.

"Oh, I disagree." His steely eyes locked onto mine. I looked back at my task. In my peripheral, he didn't raise a hand, but his muscles tensed. Muscles that were thicker, more coiled than before. "It's a game of chance, isn't it? Not talent. You were born three rooms over, and that qualifies you to rule our homeland. Tell me that's not a game of luck?"

His words scratched beneath my skin, finding raw places. I lowered my voice. "Eptah is mine. I killed no one to get it."

"Because it was given to you like a meal you didn't need to prepare."

I tied the cloth tight enough to hurt and sat back on my heels. Andros didn't move his hands, didn't attack, but the intensity in his face burned like acid.

I rubbed my fingers together, reveling in the sticky blood. I'd won here. Not him. In fact, it felt good to glare back. Let him see the same hatred in me. I wanted more of his blood coating my skin.

"You've made my life misery," I said. "I did nothing to you."

"Nothing?" he snapped. "You've taken it all and haven't even noticed."

The jacket at the tailor flashed before my mind. Then the knife I still held in one hand. I could still do it, still stab him. Feel the blade as it entered. Watch his surprise that, after so many times of being driven back, I was the one who earned the last point.

I scanned his body. Normally, I'd aim for the chest or neck but both were covered in armor. I knew what he looked like underneath, lithe and dangerous. Judging from the way the leather moved when he shifted, though, he'd gotten stronger. Could my knife pierce through his chest? No. No, it wasn't long enough. His whole body was like a strategy I struggled to understand. I'd looked at many pieces of it, knew them well, but couldn't put it all together into something defeatable. Even now, when I'd essentially won, it didn't feel like it.

He started forward. I responded without thinking, reaching out, pushing him back.

But he was dead weight. Unconscious.

I leaned him back against the wall, placing the back of my hand near his open mouth. Hot breath feathered over my blood-stained skin.

The jolt of blood urging me to fight a second ago rushed down where I didn't want it. Andros looked vulnerable, neck exposed, covered in his own blood, breathing against my skin. All that capability rendered useless. He was at my mercy. Evidently that was enough to excite me.

"Fuck," I muttered, rising and grabbing the lantern. My bulge didn't look too obvious in those loose pants. I'd been shirtless too.

Angling the blade away, I wiped some of Andros' blood on my chest. It looked good there.

Before opening the door to leave, I finally smiled.

Two days later, I stood before the same metal door. I'd given orders to clean Andros up and give him water. He had been dying, but he'd live now. A liability and an asset.

I still didn't know why I'd saved him. He deserved to die. But the rush I felt holding his life in my hands was addicting. I wanted more of that feeling. More of his blood on me.

This was better than armies clashing and warriors dying. It came down to the two of us, the ruler and rival. A pure conflict born of pure hatred. We didn't need to involve anyone else.

Especially since I held all the power here. It should have

been a familiar feeling, but this was the first time I'd really experienced it.

I stopped myself from adjusting the newly tailored jacket. "Open the door."

I was here for an interrogation, for retribution. My subjects didn't ask. They assumed I'd get what I needed and then kill him myself.

Again, the massive door swung open. Again, I held a knife and a lantern.

Andros sat chained to a bench they'd brought in to ease the doctor's work. Both manacled wrists connected to the same short end of the seat. His bare feet were free. The armor was gone. Scuffs and scratches covered his bare back and shoulder. When he turned, hair falling roguishly into his blazing eye, his chest revealed more marks. The new bandage on his head showed pink where the wound had been bloodiest, but his head wasn't covered in gore now. He looked relatively clean and upset.

"I would rather have died. Unless you want to flirt some more," he said drily. The familiar mockery didn't hold its usual laughing tone.

"You'd rather live," I said, setting down the lantern. "Thank me for saving your life."

He spat at my feet.

My mood didn't dampen. This was delicious. Having a couple days to really take in the idea that Andros himself had been captured, that the battles were over, made me buoyant.

"I see why you're angry," I said. "Isn't it horrible knowing that you can't leave without being killed?"

"Prick."

I walked closer, almost close enough to slash him with my

knife. He watched my face, not the weapon, like the strategist he was.

"How did you know we'd move on you in Lander's Creek?"

For a second, he didn't answer, then a half-smile formed. "Couldn't figure that one out?" He clucked his tongue. "And you have all that formal ruling education."

"Answer the question."

"We tracked the animals. Deathless scouts flew over the area. We knew them by their markings." He sighed. "This is basic. I could take you back to class if you want. Teach you the fucking first thing about ruling."

My cheeks burned. I hadn't been a child in a decade, but this oversight brought back scolding voices. More than once, Father said, "My gods, Teo! Andros would know how to do this." Didn't my effort mean anything?

I found Andros watching me, obviously pleased he'd hit a nerve. He sat up a little straighter, as if showing off the new muscle he'd gained. Freckles, lighter than the ones on his face, dotted the rest of his body too.

"The first thing about ruling is to protect your people," I said, letting the blade catch the light.

"Hm." He cocked his head at me with no fear in his eyes. "Are you going to ask another question?" His gaze traced the high neck on the jacket.

I knew he'd notice.

I took another step forward, testing the weight of the knife in my hand. "I could ruin that skin, carve you up while you're chained there."

"You never were good with threats. Don't say them like you want to bed me. Say them like you'll eviscerate me." The last words came out menacing and slow. A chill ran down my back.

"Like this. I'll enjoy watching you suffer as I take everything from you—every room, every title, every soldier, every friend, every privilege, even the clothes off your back."

I swallowed on a dry throat. "You told me not to seduce you." My lip rose in a snarl of disgust, but I forgot my next question.

We glared, both unmoving, the history of violence and injustice thick between us.

"Another lesson," he whispered. "Always make good."

He sprang from the bench. Chains clattered to the floor.

Body alight with surprise, I cursed. Squeezing the knife hilt, I barreled forward to meet him.

His hands met my wrists, fingers twisting to pry the knife away. His body strained toward mine. His grip hurt, but this time he didn't have his armor. Plus, he was days out of practice. It was reckless for him to attack.

I could still win.

The shock that he'd somehow freed himself crystalized into that thought. I would beat him.

I could call for soldiers to rush in to make sure of that.

No. This was the fight I wanted, the one that haunted my dreams. All this carnage had been fought over us. It was time to end it.

He changed tactics, ripping down the neck of my jacket to expose more vulnerable spots and hamstring one arm in the trapped sleeve.

I needed that mobility. Slashing at Andros' chest first, I tore off the jacket and kicked it to the side.

Andros' fighting form hadn't changed. I knew it like I knew the range of my own kick or the places my joints cracked. He was fierce, almost feral, but I knew him. This felt like release more than anything.

We grunted and tore and grasped, bruising and drawing blood. I couldn't get the knife close enough to do damage. Finally, he knocked it out of my hand. It flew to the opposite end of the cell. With him so close he practically breathed into my nose, I couldn't risk the second of focus it would take to pick it up again.

Moving together, I tried forcing him back toward the bench. I could use the restraints if I could pin him down.

Shit, he was still stronger than me.

His foot caught the back of my leg. I tripped, taking him with me.

We crashed heavily to the floor, him on top. Trapped between the hard floor and the heavy body, my lungs expelled all their breath. I wheezed, fighting to suck in air. Straw stuck to my hair as I scrambled for a better position. Andros resisted, but I used the force of the fall to roll on top of him. The bench was close, but not close enough.

Straddling his waist, I punched him in the face. Blood stuck to my fist and rolled to his upper lip. A satisfying sight. I liked having his blood on me again. It acted like the combat medals I'd never won. He kept striking and so did I until we both looked as red-streaked as Ares the god of war. Something like purpose coursed hot in my raised veins. Even as I fought to pin his hands, the thrill of it pushed my face into a fierce grin.

He bucked his hips violently, knocking me off balance and giving my groin a shock. I was hard, really hard, and he must have felt it. What the fuck was wrong with me?

For a second, I was on hands and knees. Andros' next move, grabbing my wrists so I lost all support and crashed my face into the floor, gave him the upper hand. He twisted out from underneath me. I couldn't let him stand with me down like this. He might stomp on my head, kick me, beat me with the bench, I didn't know. Suddenly our sparring sessions weren't enough to predict him. He evolved, growing more violent. Damn it, he might kill me.

I kicked out, aiming for his torso. His defined muscles flexed to absorb the blow. Because of the distance, I didn't kick him hard enough. I flew to my feet.

Before I found my balance, he was on me again, pushing me down. He'd had the same idea I did. Bench. Shackles. The wooden plank ground into my spine. When Andros sat on me, adrenaline kept me from feeling the brunt of the pain. He reached for my wrists. I fought back. My hands became moving targets.

He caught the fabric of my sleeve in a fist and forced my arm up toward the restraints. Gritting my teeth, I pulled, but all my force wasn't enough.

Then a thought. *What would Andros do?*

Fuck it.

I slipped my hand through the sleeve, pulling my arm into my shirt. The fleeting fear of having only one hand to fight lasted no time at all.

Almost before I'd decided to escape his hold that way, Andros ripped the shirt open to get to me. He always knew exactly what I'd do, what I was thinking. The tearing noise split the air. At the same time, a clear and urgent need filled every thought—to feel his reaction to my punishment. We had to fight skin to skin. All his blood and muscle against my own when I beat him. I didn't want a faraway victory. I wanted one as close I could get, to look him in the eye and breathe in his panicked panting as I demonstrated my dominance.

I bent both my thick arms so my wrists were beneath the bench. The move left me exposed. That ought to have scared me, but then I realized Andros could have hurt me worse already. Instead, he reached for what I had been planning to do: binding rather than killing. Was there a part of him that found purpose in challenging me too?

The idea didn't make me happy. If anything, it was disgust, anger, that rose up in me, but it had a sun-bright spot of rightness too. It was always going to be the two of us.

He reached for my wrists below the bench, flattening his body against mine to grab them. His bandage scraped against my own forehead. The undeniable shape of his stiff cock lay against mine. I almost gasped. Andros' mouth near my ear would have caught the sound, so I didn't.

And apparently, I didn't need to.

"You like this, huh?" Andros teased, grinding a brutal line of friction with his hips. "Like it when a real fighter puts you in your place?"

My core tightened. Every part of me felt hot.

He pulled away enough to look at my expression. He'd caught me with my mouth open, eyes half-glazed. His response of manic delight scared me more than the fight had.

I hated nothing more than to be caught in a moment of weakness. Andros had done that one too many times with his attacks, and this was different. Our rock-hard dicks sent shockwaves where they touched. My heart rammed against my ribs.

"You've wanted this," I countered as smoothly as I could. "Anything to get my attention."

My words found their mark. Andros grinned, but it wasn't the triumphant smile he gave when he won. It was the kind he plastered on to prove he didn't care.

"You can go to Abaddon," he said, thrusting ruthlessly, fucking me over my clothes.

What were we doing?

I didn't have time to think it felt wrong because, gods, *there!*, it felt right. But I wanted to do the fucking.

Andros wasn't fighting anymore, focused on forcing me to explode like some admission of defeat. Like I'd longed for him. Like I believed he was better than me.

Through the haze of blood and sweat and jagged breathing as he ground us together, I reared up and grabbed him around the middle. We fell off the bench with twin curses.

But now I was on top. He didn't fight. We were in a different competition now.

My blood-stained hand dove beneath his waistband to find his cock erect as a tree trunk. "I knew it," I muttered. My hand felt hot even after I released him to grab my own. Skin to skin. All those years of sparring and half-friendship and rivalry and blood and I hated him and I wanted him to feel this. I wanted to know that his hard-on was mine. It was because of me. When he came undone beneath me, I wanted to feel every gasp, his desperation for more, the groan of a dying man.

"Fuck you," Andros spat.

"Fuck you too."

I made good on those words, lining up our cocks so I could maximize friction. Already they were slippery with sweat and a hint of cum. I'd make Andros break.

With all the anger I felt, I rutted against him. I wanted him annihilated, and I wanted to watch.

The first clue was a flush in his cheeks. His eyes fought to stay defiantly focused on mine. His breathing went irregular. Mine came in grunts and loud exhales, but I had a job to do.

His cock rubbed the exact spot I needed, teasing my balls with his, so I stayed there, taking, taking... Oh gods, I was going to splash all over him. Gods!

I stopped, heaving in air.

Andros hadn't broken either.

Fuck.

His sculpted chest rose and fell, but it wasn't different enough from the exertion of the fight. I wanted him to whimper. To beg.

He reached up and pulled my pants down the rest of the way. My boots stayed on. Furious and too turned on to care anymore, I ripped off his too. He had two new scars on his legs since our time on the training field. My legs had never been my greatest asset. After all that sparring, I'd only ever managed to get my arms to the thickness I wanted. Andros had it all.

Then I was up, carried by my hair, and roughly tossed against the wall. Andros followed, nearly knocking the wind out of me again with his body slam.

"You want more of me, hm? I'll give you more," he hissed into my ear. I could feel all of him pressed against me. There were sticky patches of skin where I'd managed to cut him. Shit, I even felt his nipples against my back. Not to mention the rod between his legs.

His capable fingers found my ass. They were blood-slickened from his shallow wounds and slid in too easily. I released an involuntary puff of air.

"Yeah? You want me to fuck you?" He pumped his finger in, first one and then two. When he forced in a third finger, I groaned. The noise only seemed to fuel his desire to humiliate me. "That's it," he muttered, going deeper. "Bet this is the best you've had. Getting fucked in a cell by someone who hates you."

We didn't always hate each other. Resentment grew into hate. I used to envy him.

"Stop," I managed.

"You want my dick instead?"

I wanted to say no but my head was filled with yes. If I could have crawled into him and worn his skin, I would have done that too.

He pulled his fingers out. I felt empty.

"Just try," I growled. It was noncommittal, but it was a yes.

The response came immediately. Andros' length jammed against me, found the spot, forced inside.

My moan sounded like a sob. I hated myself for it, for the pleasure that lit me up. He'd hear. He'd know. But as he started pumping in, faster and faster, slapping against me with his body, hanging onto my shoulder like a friend, I stopped caring.

My dick hurt from being mashed against the wall. I was so hard I felt dizzy. From behind me came the grunts and straining sounds of sex. Sweat streamed down my back.

The hand on my shoulder became a hand around my neck. His fingers were strong.

I remembered my role. "Come for me like you've wanted to," I wheezed around his palm.

Then there it was. The whimper. He was close. And gods, I was close too.

"Want to touch it?" I asked recklessly. "Want me to come? Beg for it, you fucking bastard."

I bumped him with my ass to make him back up. My cock needed space.

It needed a hand around it.

"You gonna break first?" I egged, hardly able to gather enough breath to speak.

With a roar, he lunged for my cock. The position was awkward and released some pressure on my neck and his thrusts. I angled out of the way.

"Beg."

"You'll spill," he assured me, so close now I could smell his terrible breath. The blood on his face plastered against my cheek.

I tasted some of it on my lip. "Beg," I repeated.

We looked at each other, him inside me. Sweat mixed with the dirt and blood on his face. He'd never looked so alive.

Then he unwrapped the hand from my neck and pushed my head toward his. It was more of a bite than a kiss. Too many teeth between the soft lips. There was nothing else soft about Andros. He was made of sharp edges. He didn't pull away, and I realized I didn't want him to.

Our lips were both bleeding by the time we tore away. Warmth leaked into my beard.

Something touched my cock. A hand. Andros' hand. He pumped mercilessly, watching my face. And I watched his as he started moving his hips again, stabbing deep. I'd never been so fucking turned on.

The embarrassment I should have felt disappeared in a haze. His expressions were mine in a mirror. We were chasing something. We were both close, but, damn it, I didn't want it to stop.

When Andros' fingers tensed at the head, I clenched, unable to hold back. Loud as a war cry, Andros came behind me, startling me and pushing me over the edge as my cum splattered the wall.

Breathing heavily, I realized grit covered my chest. I was filthy. As he pulled out, I remembered the knife in the corner. If I didn't get it, he would. It lay with my jacket. What the fuck were we supposed to do now? Keep trying to kill each other?

I had no time to consider. On stupidly shaky legs, I lunged for the weapon, found the hilt, and rose to face my opponent.

He stood naked, beaming in sarcastic victory, as if he hadn't been half that fucking session. As if he hadn't come hard with me. Cum still dripped off his dick. He should have looked afraid, or at least concerned. I'd never seen Andros concerned. Determined would have been fine, since that would have shown he took me seriously as a threat. Instead, he leaned casually against the wall. My eyes slid down the ridges of his grimy body.

Focus on his face, his movements.

In minutes, my defenses had crashed to the ground. Maybe he was right to look smug.

"Get on the bench," I commanded.

"Can't wait for another round?"

I seethed. "Do it."

The most miraculous thing of the night was that he obeyed. With a light in his eye as if he knew something I didn't, he moved toward the bench. I followed him with my knife, keeping an eye on pulse points and watching for sudden movements. He spat blood before straddling the bench and sitting. His lip still bled.

Was it sick that I looked at the bite mark as a trophy? Andros, always the best fighter, the best strategist, belonged to me now. No matter what happened in the future, I had still bitten him and fucked him and made him come. I'd been in his mouth and rubbed his cock. His smell was on me. I'd crawled around inside his skin.

He reached forward, presenting his hands. To fasten the restraints, I'd have to loosen my hold on the knife. He met my eyes, a new smile crinkling the edges. All these games with him would madden me one day.

Holding eye contact, I slowly placed the knife on the ground. He didn't spring up. I cupped one shackle. He'd broken out of these before, but I didn't know how to check the mechanism. All the points were lining up on his side, even though he belonged in this dungeon.

Trying my luck, I encased his wrist in the metal bracelet and clicked it closed. His skin felt damp. He didn't struggle or move. His stillness shallowed my breath as I got ready to defend myself. The confidence emanating from him tore away mine. What good were the protections I'd built around myself—this cell, this dungeon, or these shackles? He'd best them all. He always did. Part of me wondered how he would do it.

I fastened the second shackle so both his arms attached to the bench by heavy chains. He still didn't attack, only insisted on staring at me in that unnerving way.

I rose, taking the knife with me and discovering new soreness I forgot to expect. Finding my trousers and jacket—the shirt was ripped beyond repair—I put them on and kicked Andros' dirty clothes close enough that he could re-dress too if he wanted. He didn't deserve any mercy, but he'd bowed to my wishes, so I gave him some.

I needed to clean up. Everyone would wonder what had happened to me when they saw the state of my face. Not to mention that pulling on my pants had only managed to wipe off some of the stuff off my cock.

Andros' sun-toughened face and those shrewd eyes followed me to the door. The bandage covering his head wound hung down, partially torn. He still didn't look concerned.

But I'd won, hadn't I?

"I knew you wouldn't have the stomach," he said quietly. It was the softness of the words that made me stop more than anything. Andros was loud, strident. Boastful and hateful in all he did. Never soft.

I turned. "I thought you would." I considered another insult. Discarded it. He'd left me alive, after all.

Eyes narrowing in the lantern light, he bared his teeth, almost a smile. "You'll see me again." Menace found its way back into his words.

As I left, I knew the words were true.

9
CRAVING THE ENEMY

The tables have turned. Now Andros is the one with the power.

This original story includes explicit M/M sex, strong language, bondage, dub-con, mention of war, enemies to lovers, adoration, and a toxic relationship

I promised Teo he'd see me again, and I always made good.
Before waking him, I padded to the heavy curtains at the far side of his suite and pulled one to the side. Dim moonlight fell on the blankets of his huge bed. Why did it have to be that big? Didn't he sleep alone? Our long history and recent research told me yes.

Tonight, anyway, he did. Only one shape rose beneath the covers. I didn't slant the light near his face. This moment was too delicious to spoil yet.

Teo didn't know that I'd won. It wasn't like the last time he thought he'd bested me. After the fool had saved my life, I anticipated this moment. A small number of Teo's soldiers carried the keys to the dungeon right below where I stood now. Soldiers had families. Soldiers had a price. My followers knew that and were willing to do anything to put me right here in the ruler's fortress.

Staring at the deeply breathing form of Teo, I rubbed the scar on my forehead. His forces had gotten close to killing me with that blow, but that wasn't what the raised flesh reminded me of.

With a hush of fabric, the curtain dropped. I had memorized Teo's position in the bed: face turned away, arm over the blanket, center of the mattress. I wanted his face turned toward the window—I'd checked that spot before as a potential entrance, but the glass was too thick to break easily and the panels too small for most of my troops to squeeze through.

I stalked toward the bed, blood pulsing hard through my veins. This was it, the end. Victory felt like anger. Why hadn't Teo tried harder? Why didn't he sense me in the room and attack? His vulnerability made me feel everything, like a bucket full of debris tipped out on the floor.

The childish impulse to cross over to the other side of the bed and get in his face almost won out. Instead, I drew out a strip of fabric from my pocket.

The memory of Teo wrapping the wound on my head ran through its worn grooves. In it, he crouched in front of me, shirtless, muscles flexing under the skin as he tied off the cloth. I held onto consciousness just to glare back at him. That prick had every fucking thing I wanted. He was born with it all. Nothing I did was ever enough. I could fight, I could be his friend, I could starve, I could invent new ways to spy. Divine gods, I could fuck him senseless and it would never be enough.

My mind went there next. Every time. I relived every sensation. It wasn't some poignant memory. It was a furious craving. I needed to put him in his place again, to see lust slackening his face. Our filthy sex in the dungeon filled with all the hate and all the need I'd felt since we were young only made me angrier.

He had everything I wanted.

I pounced. Looping the cloth around his head, I fitted it like a gag into his mouth.

He choked and bucked under the covers.

"Surprised to see me?" I gritted, holding him firm. The only other time my fingers had brushed his beard was in the cell. I'd hit him. I'd kissed him.

He was trying to talk, to yell, anything.

I yanked him off the bed. It was too dark to see clearly, but the vague outline of him looked shirtless again. Yes, my forearm hit bare shoulder as he tried to wrestle away.

Fuck me.

Pulling his head back so I could speak in his ear, I whispered, "I told you this would happen."

My followers were flooding the rest of the fortress now, stationing themselves at all the exits. My midnight raid had worked even better than I expected.

Thrashing, Teo elbowed me in the ribs.

I grunted and forced him face down on the bed. Our combined body weight pinned one of his thick arms down.

"I wouldn't do that," I hissed. "I was deciding whether to show you mercy."

He smelled like warm, clean skin. Fuck him. And this position... shit. We had to move. I managed to tie the fabric around his head like he'd done to me.

"Get up. We're going for a walk."

Hauling him upright, I forced him toward the door. Light poured out when he opened it. Even though he was listening to me, the easy way he opened the door reeked of entitlement. This was his fortress, his province, his everything.

My guess had been right—he wore nothing but soft, loose-fitting pants slung low on his hips. I usually slept in partial armor.

He turned his head to look at me. If he needed to confirm my identity, he was more of a fool than I thought. Maybe he had a primal need to know who pulled him out of bed in the middle of the night to take everything that was his.

In the moment our eyes locked, I smiled. For the final time, I'd won.

He sighed, nearly relaxed. It was as if he knew where we were going. I couldn't decide whether I was glad he acknowledged his position as my prisoner. Shouldn't we keep fighting?

A couple turns and a skinny hallway later, we reached a new room. I pushed Teo inside and closed the door.

Inside was a much smaller bedchamber, no tapestries or four-posters. No windows, even. Lanterns flickered in sconces along the walls.

"Do you know where we are?" I asked, even though he couldn't answer.

I allowed another smirk to cross my features. Teo, here, gagged. This was a good day.

He raised an eyebrow as if to say he didn't care. His brown eyes skipped from my face to objects in the room. He was looking for a way to escape, to defend himself.

In the silence, he kept scanning and searching everywhere but at me.

"Look at me!" I bellowed.

His eyes snapped back to mine. His mouth stretched almost comically around the gag. I'd thought about bringing more fabric to bind his wrists and ankles—that would have been smart—but I wanted victory so decisive that I didn't need it.

Our encounter in the dungeon happened a year ago. A couple days after that, my followers helped me escape. I expected Teo to track me down, but he never did. All my vigilance to prepare for him, all the gnawing on details of that night that could have given him a clue to find me, all the stress I suffered about whether I'd kill him after all... it was all for nothing. I laid siege to the city and I still didn't matter enough to confront in person.

I was an idiot to think that our rutting, sweaty hate sex changed a damn thing. All it did was distract me at the wrong moments.

I exhaled slowly. My bitterness needed to funnel here, now. Because I'd won. The fortress was mine. And, at this moment, Teo was mine too.

"This room, Teo, is where I was born. I started here, you remember?"

We were the same age, but he should have retained some information about me. We only grew up and trained together for years.

"I thought it was the perfect place to tell you my news."

Teo glared back now, not breaking eye contact. Good. His hair had gotten longer since I saw him last. It fell practically to his shoulders. Any fighter should have known to keep it short.

Satisfaction welled up again, cooling some of my anger. I cocked my head. "I've taken the fortress. I've taken Eptah. It's over now. I know it's been difficult for you." The last statement felt like a joke, so I chuckled.

Teo barreled forward, aiming for my midsection. We crashed against the wall. A picture in a frame teetered and crashed to the floor.

I grappled with his bare back. I wore quieter clothes for this mission, better for moving uninhibited, so the blow hit me with more force than when I wore my chest plate. So I was in pain, yes, but relieved too. Teo fought back instead of accepting like the passive heir I feared he was. His arms wrapped around me.

Teo's fighting style was blunt and obvious. I'd fought with him enough times to predict what he would do. In seconds, I held him in a headlock. More than once, as teenagers, he'd refuse to yield until he passed out. I liked him more for that. It was something I would have done, if I ever had to.

I felt him struggling to breathe against the crook of my arm. "When I say I've taken the fortress, I mean no one loyal to you is within screaming distance. Now, are you ready to listen?"

He stopped struggling.

I released him.

"You always insist on throwing yourself at me," I said, my mood darkening again as I said it. "If you were someone else, I might get the wrong idea."

Teo ripped off the gag, stretching his mouth and throwing the cloth to the side. "You're bluffing," he seethed.

My cheek crinkled in amusement. "Would you like a tour of my fortress to make sure?"

"Fuck..." he muttered. A line creased his torso where his sheet had folded under him.

"Is that an order?"

When he turned his blazing gaze on me again, I could see the dungeon in his eyes. He remembered. Why he didn't do a damn thing about it was a mystery. I let my eyes drop to his chest, the gentle swell of his pecs and stomach. Compared to him, I was tough as a piece of gristle.

His lip curled in disgust.

"If you're sure," I said lightly. "Isn't it strange to be here like this?" I looked around the room. "How does it feel to lose everything you didn't work for?"

"Let me out or kill me," he growled. The tone was severe, but his eyes were fearful or sad.

"Hmm. No. I've imagined this moment." I advanced on him until we stood a breath away. He didn't retreat. "On your knees."

He scoffed, even smiling.

"I've already taken your province. Do you want me to take more? Where do you think all those soldiers and servants are if they're not in the fortress?"

His smile faded.

"I said, kneel."

Conflict evident in his eyes, he stood his ground.

"No one's here to see," I goaded, moving even closer. My pulse began to throb.

Finally, he backed up a step and lowered slowly to his knees. Fuck, it was a pretty sight. He looked furious, but my cock didn't care.

I hinged forward at the waist to seethe into his ear the words I'd practiced nearly every day for a year. "Now that's where you belong. On your knees, at my feet."

"Spare my people." He said it mildly, as if my compliance were a given. The arrogance to assume that any outcome he wanted would automatically happen...

"Maybe," I said carelessly. As I straightened, I caught his eyes roaming to places on my body where they had no business. Fierce excitement thrilled through me. It was almost enough to make me forget what an entitled shit he was.

He looked at the door next. No one was coming to save him.

For a split second, I pictured myself bursting in. Teo's assumption was right. Someone was coming to rescue him. It was me. It would always be me.

I shook off the bizarre fantasy. I was no one's savior, least of all Teo's. Our rivalry would end in blood, and we both knew it.

"You want this?" I asked, palming my crotch. "I shouldn't be surprised, after last year." I rolled my eyes.

His expression said revulsion but his mouth said nothing.

"I bet you haven't had a good fuck since. Can't stop thinking about me behind you, fucking up into your ass. I even told you how much I hate you and you still lapped it up like a dog."

Teo's breathing grew heavier. Then confidence invaded his eyes again. "You'd wanted to do that for a long time. I bet you'd give up the fortress if I sucked your dick."

The suggestion hurled me into lust so fast it took my mind a second to catch up. Teo offered to suck my dick. Was he offering? Was he as turned on as I was? I glanced down to see a slight bulge growing in his pants. Oh my gods...

But he wasn't offering. He was making a point.

"You think highly of your abilities," I quipped. "If you want to show them off, I won't stop you."

My heart rammed against my ribs. The lighting was bright enough in here that he could see my skin heating up if he ever paid that much attention.

I shouldn't have said anything. Normally, I knew exactly what to say and how to move. I focused on objectives and acted accordingly. If earning a victory meant being ruthless, I would do it.

But here...

I brought Teo here to lord over him. I craved the sight of him kneeling before me as I announced that Eptah was mine. I hadn't allowed myself to think far beyond that. Plans always turned into memories which turned into furtive sessions alone with myself in my tent.

Teo seemed to be out of words for a minute, because he didn't respond. Then he said, "For the fortress?"

I laughed. "No! Not for the fortress. Don't be an idiot. I've won, Teo. I'm keeping everything." I bent toward him again, relishing how serious he looked. As if I'd forfeit a province for a blowjob, even one from my rival, which I'd admit would have been satisfying.

"I can get it back," he said in an undertone.

"We both know that's not true." It was a desperate gambit not to yield, just like he refused to when we fought hand to hand. I won those fights too. "Don't embarrass yourself. You're already on your knees for me." The reminder made me harder. Hard meant stupid, self-indulgent. I wanted to grind against his face.

I stepped closer. He could undo the clasp on my pants if he wanted to, pull out my dick, suck it into his mouth. I wouldn't have stopped him.

In a fluid movement, he grabbed my knees. I fell like a tree, the impact rattling from my tailbone up my spine.

A laugh burst from my mouth. Resistance at last. I needed something definite, and even Teo on his knees didn't complete my conquest somehow. This felt better. Fighting or full submission. Nothing in between.

When Teo vaulted to straddle me and hold me down, I realized how this ended. I had known for a long time that ours was an absolute rivalry. I'd kill him. Unless he chose to belong to me.

"Fucker," he hissed, aiming blows at my face. One made contact. I heard no crunch of bone but my eyes automatically streamed.

I twisted, knocking him off me. Pressing his neck against the ground, I got on top of him instead. His soft, naked torso rose with quick breaths. "It's over, Teo." I blinked the wetness from my eyes. The shock of pain to my face had already subsided a little.

I couldn't quite manage the easy grin I meant to give him, showing my canines in a grimace instead. Fuck him. I'd kill the entitled son of a bitch, but I didn't want to.

"Why are you being so stubborn, hm? You know I won this just like I beat you all those other times." I shook his neck. He fought for breath.

If I didn't conquer Teo, the other victories meant nothing.

"I need you to say it," I said. Malice dripped from the words.

I relaxed my hold so he could speak.

"Monster."

With a growl, I smacked his head against the ground. "I'd be a better ruler than you and you know it!"

"Why do you give a fuck what I say?" he burst out, eyes ablaze. "You're in here torturing me. For what? I won't yield to you."

I narrowed my eyes. Maybe he was right. When I sat up straight, allowing him space to fill his lungs, something blunt touched me in the lower back.

My lips curled. "I can make you." A slight rotation of my hips made my back brush against his cock again. Teo's lips parted.

Did he think about that night too? How I hated him and fucked him until he was a whimpering mess?

Did he want that again as bad as I did?

I was fucked up. I knew that. And I didn't care.

Impulsively, I reached behind me and groped for his dick. There it was through the fine fabric of his pants, growing harder as I stroked it down to the balls and back up.

"Tell me to stop, Teo," I goaded. But his eyes had slammed shut as if my touch pained him. "Have you waited for me every night? I bet you wish I'd fuck you against this wall. You want my dick in your mouth? Gonna be good for me?"

I barely knew what I was saying anymore. The feeling of Teo's hard on in my fist as I kneaded the length of him made me feverish.

I lowered my voice. "I bet you touch yourself when you think of me, don't you, you sick fuck?" A noise, almost like a whine, shot from between Teo's lips. My pace quickened. I didn't want to do this with my hand behind my back anymore. "You know I have everything you want." I was confessing too much. Watching his face was delicious but I had to stop talking.

Twisting so I sat backward on his chest, I finally saw Teo's stiff cock tenting his pants high. I grabbed it again, this time diving beneath the waistband.

Teo cried out. *Fuck fuck fuck.* "You can't..." he gasped.

"Can't what?"

His large hands slid around my thighs, still perched on either side of his chest. I was already so turned on I ached, but that motion made me desperate. He might have been trying to get me off him. That, or he was widening my legs to do something between them. I didn't give a fuck.

I fumbled madly at the front of my pants to pull out my sensitive length. It matched Teo's.

"Yes, I can," I managed and stretched out to lower my mouth to the head. I'd scooted down so far that Teo's beard teased the root of my dick. When I spat on his cock and fed its hard length past my lips, Teo made a chorus of sounds. Choking, sobbing, cursing, begging sounds that made me utterly delirious.

I rocked my hips to get friction against whatever part of Teo I could touch. His neck maybe, but then those same large hands scrabbled with my weight, repositioning me. He wasn't going to…?

Wet warmth slid down my shaft. Shock and need hit me with so much force I shouted. I was in Teo's mouth. The danger filed past my mind, but it was so stuffed with lust I didn't care. Teo could bite off my dick. But he was pulsing his tongue around it instead. And I couldn't breathe, couldn't think. He thrust upward into my mouth and I thrust downward into his and *holy fuck!*

This would be an ecstatic way to kill him, suffocated by my cock in his throat. And fuck if it wasn't an ecstatic way to die.

Shit! The way he sucked made me clench. He was trying to get me off.

He was trying to prove I'd break first.

Did I care?

I lifted my grinding hips, slipping out from between his lips, and rolled to the side. Desire burned beneath my skin like lightning, all that energy ready to lash out. I could barely keep from shaking.

Teo looked at me in a wary daze, his lips wet and pink. He sat up, but all that did was show off his body with all that give to it.

On a dry mouth, I said, "I said you wanted to suck me off."

Dick still out, he caught his breath. The moment turned strangely serious. He didn't strike out. Neither did I. I had nothing else to prove. I was just biding my time before the inevitable final play in our lifetime-long struggle.

"You want me, don't you?" Teo asked it with too much seriousness. He wasn't mocking. He was concerned that he might be right.

He looked at me when he said it. That was the worst part. He didn't scan the room, but looked right into my eyes.

A bolt shot through me at the question. I didn't owe him an answer. He didn't care about me, and I didn't want to think about him. He was an arrogant prick, soft, handed everything in life. He was born like *that* and then given all he wanted, even though I would have made a more competent ruler. His troops had killed some of mine and had almost killed me. But then Teo saved my life, and we...

I spoke in insults and commands. Since neither fit, I didn't answer right away and hated myself for it. Finally, I settled on, "I hate you and what you stand for." I cleared my throat. "I wanted what you got for free, and now I have it."

I had the province of Eptah. I had the ruler's residence and stronghold. Tonight, I had taken power and titles and everything Teo owned. The only thing missing was my enemy. It should have been easy to end him and begin the life I'd been striving for since I was a teenager, held back by the very room where we sat. Teo was born an heir. I was born a soldier. It should have been easy.

But he had everything I wanted.

By the end of the night, he'd be dead or he'd be mine.

My heart thumped heavy in my chest as I regarded him. His deep-set eyes showed a hint of fear. He wasn't completely ignorant, then. After our scramble on the floor, his brown hair was bed-messy. My gaze slid down to the thick arms propping himself up.

We'd fought hundreds of times, one-on-one or in battles. I always had the upper hand. Teo, no matter how he tried, wasn't as strong, as quick, as inventive. In a fight, I would win, just as I had tonight. That didn't feel risky. And I thrived on risk. Was this risk too much, though?

I pictured dice that could decide a game.

Dead or mine.

This would determine my path. I felt lightheaded with adrenaline.

Reaching out, I grabbed the back of Teo's head and kissed him.

He snarled into my mouth. I ate the sound, rough, crowding in closer. I'd crossed the line. There was no undoing what I'd done, so I wanted all of him, *needed* all of him. My fingers knotted in his hair as I crawled over him again. He sat up fully now, pushing back as if this were another contest. Who could press in harder? Who could get the upper hand?

He leaned in, tasting salty and musty. No pulling away. Was this why he sucked my dick, why he kissed me back, so he could match me stride for stride without saying anything pained him? Was it another form of not admitting defeat?

Or did he think about that godsdamned time when I slammed him against the cell wall and took him hard?

Well, then. If he let me do it before…

I pressed myself flush against his chest, feeling its soft swells. Hooking my fingers in the fabric of his pajamas, I yanked them down to get them off. Everything off.

The position was awkward. I'd have to move for him to get naked.

I broke the kiss and jumped up. He gazed up at me, dumb and desiring. I bared my teeth at him and hauled him up by his hair so we were both standing.

Before I could even crush my lips to his again, Teo ripped at my clothes.

"Yes," I breathed, kicking off my pants and letting him pull my shirt over my head. It was a compromising position. All of this was. I made myself a target for him and now he had extra ways to slay me.

Bu he didn't stab while I was blinded by fabric with arms trapped in sleeves. The worst he did was scratch with short fingernails as he squeezed handfuls of my flesh. A bite to my lip dripped blood. As long as I could consume him, he could scratch all he liked.

We shoved each other toward the small bed. Delirious with want, I hardly noticed he pushed me over first.

"Fuck you," he said between jagged puffs of air. His legs lined up with the back of mine.

I kicked him off, standing and shoving his knees from under him. He fell forward on the bed, ass toward me.

"You missed me," I said and spat on my throbbing erection. Moving fast, I speared him from behind. He was tight, contracting around me. Sinking into him again filled me with a frenzy.

A noise like an ache shuddered through him at my intrusion. Curses followed.

"That's right," I huffed. "You dreamed about this." I knifed my hips forward. Holding him down, I moved faster. Sweat bloomed on my skin. He stroked my cock with his body.

Already close, I paused, still inside. I had to calm down. Had to think. The impulse to consider my next move dug so deep that it stilled me in the middle of fucking my conquered enemy.

Self-preservation. Improvement. *Prove you're better than they are.*

I did. No one but stubborn bastards like Teo could even try to dispute that. Now I could try letting go of my wire-sprung control. At least while we were in this room.

Leaning down, I brushed hair from his face. I couldn't read his expression. Time for another risk.

"Yes," I bit out. "And you never fucking noticed."

He'd asked the question minutes ago, but by the way his eyes widened, I knew he understood.

"Oh."

My lip curled, brow furrowing. "Oh?" I began moving my hips again, puncturing deep.

Teo's heartbeat pulsed heavily enough for me to feel it under my hand as I held him down. At my movement, his expression became absent, focused.

It was the expression I saw behind my eyelids, the lustful abandon, open and obscene, when I smacked into him, balls deep, as a prisoner. Now he was my prisoner. And he still looked like that before he came.

I straightened and pumped into him. The landscape of his back looked like a place to sleep. It looked like a map showing where to slip in a knife.

My flat belly tightened. I wasn't ready to end it. Not yet.

With a gasp, I pulled out, painfully hard. That was close.

Teo whipped around. The sight must have been laughable—me, shuddering, chest heaving, erect as a post, having confessed my darkest secret.

But he didn't laugh. He simply asked, "Why?" His gaze went liquid, as if he'd just said the dirtiest thing.

It felt like the dirtiest thing. All the reasons. And the way he looked at me. Fuck.

"Why?" I scoffed.

Teo rolled onto his back and sat up. His dick pointed up at me.

Unease crawled through my belly. Confidence had never been my problem. I didn't get nervous. Now I was acting like some godsdamned tongue-tied teenager. Why couldn't we just fuck and get on with it?

Look at you, I wanted to say. *The eyes, the arms, the tongue, the voice, the feet. The power I never inherited. The way you'd pass out before yielding. The way I hate and need you more than the blood in my body.*

Teo's hand inched toward his balls, like he was waiting for me to say something.

I ground my teeth together. "I used to go to the suna," I rasped. I didn't need to clarify that I meant the place where his father's cult gathered. "I prayed to you and you gave me nothing."

For about a year, the visits became habit. I never told anyone. I might have been nineteen at the time. Young. After a sparring match, I'd head to the suna, pour out a drink offering to the God-King, and go inside. Most were there to worship Lord Rex, Teo's father. I bypassed his statue and lit a candle for Teo. A quick drop to a knee and then I'd leave. Habit. Adoration. And I never got a damn thing from it.

Teo's body responded with a flush. "You prayed to me," he repeated, barely audible. His fingers teased himself.

What were we doing? Why was I telling him any of this?

But his motion and obvious arousal hypnotized me. How desperate could I make him?

"I wanted to take you in the training grounds. I arranged extra sessions so you would touch me."

Teo's hand closed around his shaft and he began stroking.

My stomach flipped. He flashed a self-aware, guilty look up at me, but he didn't stop. "Your body kept me up at night," I continued.

A tremble shook his veined arms. Teo was trembling.

I could make him shake more. My chest hurt from the heavy speed of my pulse.

"I wanted to think about other things, but the smallest part of you would hurl me back. You'd just be walking around a corner, but I'd stare at that corner and picture your shoulders. I'd picture you on your knees."

Teo whimpered. I wanted to drink the sound.

My recklessness crested like a wave. "I want everything you have."

Still holding his dick, Teo shot awkwardly to his feet, pressing his lips to mine. His damp chest met my own at a thousand burning points. I recognized his next wrestling move, even one-armed.

For the first time, I let him win.

He forced me down on my stomach. Those big hands kneaded my ass and shot a dose of blood to my already straining dick. I growled, on the verge of losing any shred of control. I'd never felt so feral. Teo's cock stabbed in, sure and deep as a blade.

I barely had enough room for him. No one else had ever taken me like this. I wouldn't have let them. So I was tight and painful and bleeding and *fuuuuck*...

Wild with the feel of Teo inside, I snapped, "More!"

He moved faster, holding onto my hips.

"More!" It felt like a mantra, a prayer. "More!"

Teo groaned, grinding deeper, hands slipping against sweaty skin. He finally pushed far enough that his body hit my ass every time. No war music had ever raised my blood higher than that rhythmic slap. His balls hit mine. I pushed back against him to get deeper, deeper.

We were growling, huffing. It was all the torture and adoration I craved.

"More!"

With a yell, Teo obeyed, thrusting with dizzying speed.

"Everything... you have." Speaking became almost impossible. My voice creaked. All my air was gone as I braced myself.

With a broken, delicious, dying moan, Teo shot hot cum inside me. When he stumbled back, I thought I felt him tremble again.

I was leaking, so hard I could barely see, but I hadn't let myself explode yet. I didn't want to turn around. I didn't want the fight to end.

But I had to face this, had to face *him*.

Gods, what had I said?

Teo stood looming over the bed, streaked with sweat. I couldn't read his expression beyond post-coital exhaustion. I sat up.

"Have fun?" I asked, trying to regain some version of myself that wasn't flayed open by honesty.

His eyes dropped to my long hard on, oozing cum. "What did you pray for?"

"It doesn't matter."

"Tell me."

I tried for a smirk but didn't quite reach it. "I don't have to tell you anything."

He pushed hair out of his face. How did he make that look so sexy? "But this is your last chance."

So he knew that too.

Dead or mine.

He set his jaw. I wanted him angry, not serious. I didn't want him to have the power to pry me open. Gods, war was better than this.

"It wasn't words most of the time. I'd just... think of something."

There went Teo's bedroom eyes again. I was still sitting there barely able to control my raging boner, so it was better to turn him on again than not. I had to finish sometime.

"I'd picture your foot or your jaw." Fuck, this was horrible. I shouldn't have been saying any of this. I'd never told anyone before. If my followers knew any of this, I'd be done.

But then...

Teo lowered to his knees.

I stared at him and he stared back.

In monotone, I continued. "Sometimes I'd picture the bulge in your pants. Or your eyes."

He caressed my leg. Caressed it. What the fuck? My anticipation shot so high I started shaking.

Fuck fuck fuck!

"And I'd..." But I had no idea what words were at that point. Teo obviously got off on praise, but my whole body already praised him more than I wanted to. It was an ache, a need.

Teo's thick arm wrapped around my bare back while his other hand pushed gently against my knee to open my thighs.

On his knees.

Face lowering.

He licked me from base to tip. I shook violently, past the point of caring. Every particle of skin was so sensitive that the brush of his beard or the sigh of his breath was enough to make me squirm. I'd never squirmed for anyone before, but Teo was on his knees for me, slurping me up like a treat, like he'd wanted to worship me like I did him, and I'd happily die like this. Shame was nothing. This was everything.

All my focus followed the movements of his tongue and hands, the seconds when he flicked his gaze to mine, the way he sucked my balls into his mouth. I didn't say a fucking word.

Today would replace the dungeon in my filthiest dreams.

When Teo closed his lips over the tip again, my hand lashed out to grab his hair to hold his head there. Arching and needy, I thrust into his mouth. He let me. His hands were free and could have tried to stop me. I pushed further, punishing, taking. Incoherent sounds burst out of me. After only a few thrusts, I seized, out of self-control, and let a loud, messy orgasm wring my body dry.

Gasping for air, I released my grip on Teo's hair. He licked his lips and, gods, had he ever looked so good?

"Now that's... a sight... I like to see." I tipped his chin up toward me. "Right where you should be."

"I'll get the province back," he said, but he didn't have the same bitterness as before.

I grinned. "No, you won't."

It was a game now. A game with people's lives, sure, but we never claimed we weren't fucked up.

"From the inside," he declared, standing and searching for his discarded pajama bottoms.

"So I'll know your every move?"

"You won't."

"I'm better than you."

Teo gave me a knowing look. Shit. I'd given him too much to use against me.

"You can't stage a coup if I'm always watching," I said.

He pulled on his pants. "We'll see." A half-smile crept onto his face. "Fuck you."

I ran my tongue over my teeth and smiled back. "Sounds weak coming from a defeated enemy." With a wink, I stood, searching for my own clothes.

Maybe one day I'd kill him, but it sure as fuck wouldn't be today. *Let the games continue.*

"I have business to finalize," I said. "Above your level. When I get back, stay on the far side of the bed."

Since his suite and his bed were so large, why not keep my worst enemy close?

Teo frowned, then chuckled wryly in understanding. I let myself take in the swell of his hip and the crinkle of his eyes. It had been ages since I'd really looked at him like this. It felt like the mental pictures I'd indulged in at the suna when I dipped to a knee before the candle, rather than my daydreams of a gory blade between his ribs.

Allowing Teo freedom of movement was a risk, but, as today showed with ample proof, sometimes the biggest risks paid off.

THANK YOU!

Thank you for reading *Secrets and Midnights*! Please consider leaving a review. Reviews help authors like me get found by more readers.

Sign up for my newsletter to read *Wings and Blindness*—an Eros and Psyche remix that asks what would happen if Psyche were sent to kill Eros from the beginning...

THANK YOU!

This first book in the Deathless Love series welcomes you to the Eight Realms, where danger and desire lurk in every corner, and mythology isn't quite as you remember it.

Join the Foxy newsletter and read this book FREE!

READ MORE BY ZORA FOX

Fae and Shadow duology
    End of the Forest
    Trapped by the Fae

Deathless Love—novels
    Wings and Blindness
    Flowers and the Far Realm
    Flame and Warpaint
    Temptation and Tridents

Deathless Love—novellas
    Storm and Sanctuary
    Full Moons and Vampires
    Candle Wax and Sunlight

Deathless Love—erotic short stories
    Lovers and Monsters

www.ingramcontent.com/pod-product-compliance
Lightning Source LLC
LaVergne TN
LVHW090041080526
838202LV00046B/3915